I0771284

DOPPELGÄNGER

DOPPELGÄNGER

SHAWN STERN

A Division of RÖK Publishing, Inc.

DOPPELGÄNGER

Cover Art by: Ben Kiser
Author Photo by: Jeb Corliss

For more information:
INVADER PRESS
A Division of RÖK Publishing, Inc.
30745 P.C.H. #343, Malibu, California 90265
or
Visit our website at:
www.rokpublishing.com
Email:
info@rokpublishing.com

ISBN-13: 978-0-9849266-1-9
Library of Congress Control Number: 2012901190

Printed in the U.S.A.
First edition, January 2014

The text type was set in Baskerville.

For Shane Casey,

*My friend and artist. You made every story I ever wrote into
something infinitely more interesting than my humble words ever
could.*
I never had the opportunity to say goodbye or thank you.
Until now…

Invention, it must be humbly admitted, does not consist in creating out of void but out of chaos.

– Mary Shelley

We know what we are, but not what we may be.

– William Shakespeare

FACT & FICTION

The following is a combination of both fact and fiction. This author has chosen to leave it up to the reader to decipher and locate the difference.

It began with the Singularity.

By the beginning of the 21st century, most people had not realized the full extent artificial intelligence (A.I.) and bio-genetic engineering had permeated human existence. 'Primitive' A.I. began as machine intelligence that equaled or exceeded human capacity for precise functions. On a daily basis, computers did everything from complicated tasks like flying and landing airplanes (fly-by-wire), diagnosing diseases, and guiding complex industrial processes, to the mundane acts of sending an email or talking on cell phones. This soon became the primary way in which we communicated and socially interacted. Our shared use of intelligent systems had become so common place that nobody knew what was actually happening.

It was estimated that approximately ten quadrillion calculations per second would begin to provide a functional equivalent to the human brain and by the end of the second decade of the new millennium, machine intelligence possessed the full range of human intelligence.

It was only a matter of algorithms in order to reverse engineer the human brain and understand the complex pattern recognition that took place within our minds.

The spatial and temporal brain scanning tools that were built identified and mapped out individual connections between neurons and observed their firing across all of the various regions of the human brain. Mathematical models were built of the entire cerebral cortex and programmers conducted simulations that matched them.

These simulations allowed Van, a computer scientist, in Palo Alto, California to write the source code and design some of the most powerful machines ever created. Soon, recursive self-improvement allowed the new computers to create and design yet even greater machines with exponentially more capabilities than the previous ones. Moore's Law had exploded right in front of Van and she was among the vanguard guiding the direction of this new technological frontier. Van's programs were beginning to demonstrate the ability to recognize patterns on a par with human beings.

It was not long before she was 'enlisted' into the program, arrested and detained was more like it, along with all of her machines and equipment. And despite her initial protests, it would be the arcane Director Gray who guided the direction her work and new 'intelligent' machines would take from that day forth.

Simultaneously, on the other side of the world in Tel Aviv, Israel, nanotechnology was allowing scientists like neuro-geneticist Jacob Daedalus to build vast numbers of tiny machines at the molecular level. The application of the new robust A.I., combined with nanotechnology, created the first blood-cell-sized robots he affectionately referred to as nano-bots.

The new nano-bot technology, like that of the genetically modified food we were consuming, soon outpaced government legislation. Private corporations, unbeknownst to the world, released trillions of these nano-bots into the human population. Trillions of these tiny biological machines were traveling in the entire human populations' bloodstream, communicating with one another and transmitting information to the individuals controlling them.

That was the first project Dr. Daedalus worked on for Director Gray. The next project would have even greater implications on the population.

Without anybody knowing it the Singularity had begun, and the world would never be the same.

BOOK I
DOPPELGÄNGER

Doppelgänger is a German term that translates to "double goer," or "double walker."

A Doppelgänger is an entity somewhere in the world that is indistinguishable from another person. Even when taking into consideration the billions of combinations in an individual human's DNA and the immense population on earth, it remains possible that at least some people have identical physical doubles.

The advent of cloning sciences, genetic manipulations and technologies has only fueled imaginations and raised religious, moral, or ethical questions concerning the possibility of genetic body-doubles walking among us.

In literature, we have seen the Doppelgänger as a shadow entity of a living human being, an "evil twin" causing mischief and mayhem, or used as a metaphor and/or allegory to explore an individual's own personal identity.

Whatever the reality of the Doppelgänger, many people, including figures of fame and history, have reportedly claimed to have run into their own duplicate.

Doppelgängers are often considered to be an evil omen or the harbinger of death.

PROLOGUE
PIECES OF YOU

Evangeline Murray, her friends liked to call her Van, was twenty-seven years old when she learned she was dying. Locked in her own private war with cancer, and the enigmatic disease was winning.

Van was recovering from her fourth surgery since finding the tumor six and a half months ago. She was grateful at least to have not broken down to tears in front of the oncologist the program had provided for her. The doctor, a man who was proficient enough at his job, lacked any kind of warmth or human empathy.

Under normal circumstances Van would have preferred a female doctor, but had no choice in the matter due to the fact that she, like most of her research team, were being sequestered to the program's classified location until the completion of the P.R.I.M.E. project. This left Van with no option but to accept whatever medical treatment the program provided her with.

The program had recently changed its direction due to an unexpected outcome in their experiment. For months, Van had been facing a moral dilemma over these new directives and their associated implications. However, with this new medical revelation of her imminent demise, Van had made up her mind. Still, she was going to need some time to implement her plan into action. And she was going to need some help.

"How much time do I—?" But her voice broke before she could finish the sentence.

"Six months," the doctor continued her sentence for her with cold formality. She would be dead within one year from her original diagnosis.

Despite the very real prospect of facing her own mortality, Van smiled to herself at this small bit of good news. She would need only three months for what she planned to do next.

Two months and three weeks later…

I still have enough time. Van tried to convince herself as she sprinted down the laboratory's long corridor. Her white lab coat flapped behind her like a cape, having been torn in half from her violent fight with Director Gray in the containment lab. She had managed to knock him unconscious and tie him up in the lab, but not before he had injected her with something.

Van's running was causing what she believed to be a neurotoxin to race through her blood stream. She knew the poison would perform its lethal task with efficiency and certainty, but she did not care. Van assumed that she would be dead soon, perhaps within minutes, but she was determined to save the infant cradled in her arms.

Van's heart promised to burst from her chest as she heaved her petite body at the heavy air-pressurized doors, forcing the locking mechanism to give way. The agony of the impact momentarily blinded her, but still, she kept running. She was thankful for the pain. She hoped it would allow her to stay conscious and alert long enough to deliver the baby to safety.

Mercifully, she soon found the man she had been searching for, Dr. Jacob Daedalus, the program's lead scientist and Van's best friend and mentor. He was standing by the antique vending machine near the lounge, digging into the pockets of his Harris Tweed suit for some money. He was the only one she trusted with her precious package.

Hearing a noise behind him, the scientist turned in time to say, "Van, what in heaven's name–?" before she rushed into his arms. He noticed immediately by her feverish pallor that something was very wrong and that she was cradling a baby.

"Help me?" she pleaded, thrusting the small infant into the man's arms, before collapsing to the ground.

She felt more of whatever it was that Director Gray had injected her with. Her vision was already being impaired. Van assumed paralysis, respiratory failure and death would soon come next.

"Please help me save the boy."

Overcome and surprised, the man could do nothing but accept the squirming little bundle. Oddly, the infant looked up at him with calm gecko green eyes, as if to say, "Hello there Dr. Daedalus, and how is your day going?" Despite the chaos around it, the child's calm face regarded him with wide-eyed perspicacity and remained silent.

Briefly transfixed by the child's tranquility, the man's eyes eventually lifted from the baby, back to his dear friend and colleague. She was lying on her side, fading in and out of consciousness. Dying.

"What we did…" the woman whispered between shallow breathes, "none of us imagined… even you had doubts… and we did fail in what we initially set out to do." She choked violently trying to catch her breath before she could continue, "Created him in-stead– the P.R.I.M.E., and he's a beautiful disaster, don't you think?" she asked gazing at the baby, a deep love resolved in her eyes.

"Van, for God's sake, what have you done? Please tell me this is not what I think it is? We weren't going to evacuate the child for another two weeks. There are still preparations to be made. I'm not ready!" the man asked already knowing and fearing the answer.

"It's a he not an it, Jacob" Van corrected, ignor-ing the man's questions, "and yes, HE possesses abili-ties–strange and fantastic abilities. But he is a child and you know better than anyone what they plan to use him for." It was becoming increasingly more difficult to speak, her time was almost gone.

Van was rambling in a kind of delirium but Jacob Daedalus knew she was referring to the rumors of how Director Gray wanted to weaponize the child and hide him from the other twelve regions. When the P.R.I.M.E. first began to display extraordinary abilities it soon became obvious that Director Gray had plans to keep the child for himself. Leveraging his new weap-on against the other twelve region Directors of the Cabal and tipping the precarious balance of power.

"Van, I can't do this." Daedalus tried to reason

with her. They had been planning the boy's extraction from the lab for weeks, but it was Van not he who was supposed to actually take the child. Something must have gone terribly wrong for Van to have deviated from the plan so drastically. "Perhaps we should--".

But she cut him off, "Jacob, listen to me." Her eyes focusing into his, "I didn't set an upper-limit to the algorithm. He's open ended Jacob. There might not be a limit to his power." She was beginning to shake all over now. "I'm so sorry Jacob, after all our time together, I never got to tell you who I really am, but there's no time now. Someone must protect him. If Director Gray is planning to use him to take over the other twelve regions, he will want him back at all costs. It's only a matter of time before they come after the child. After you–" She warned with the little strength she had left. She began gasping violently for a breath that would not come. She could feel her body going numb in the arms of the man whom she had trusted and respected for so long.

Thinking about the Director, with his cold steel colored eyes, sent a chill down Dr. Jacob Daedalus's spine. "Evangeline, you were supposed to take the child, not me. I was going to use my clearance to get you out of the facility." The man paused, looking down again at the baby. "Besides, I'm a scientist not some baby-minder. I can't very well take care of this child. What do you expect me to do?" However, Jacob's words fell on deaf ears.

"It has to be you." Time was not on her side now. Only the last bit of adrenaline coursing through her veins and sheer force of will allowed her to still speak. "I destroyed our notes and all of the backups. Without you and me they won't be able to duplicate the experiment." She tried to catch her breath before continuing, "If you can find him, tell my father what we have done." Her strength was almost gone now, "But no matter what, watch over the child. Protect him. Love him… I can't anymore—" She let out a small gasp of air before her last word fully left her lips. Her eyes locked on the child once more, before closing.

Protecting him, even in her own death. Jacob Daedalus thought to himself while trying and failing miserably, to stifle the tears that were welling up in his eyes.

Dr. Evangeline "Van" Murray had worked with him on the project since its inception for the last three years and was probably among its most gifted members. Their initial experiment had failed miserably but instead they had accidentally created the P.R.I.M.E. in its place. She had been the one to design and implement most of the safeguards and limitations to what became the P.R.I.M.E. program in order to ensure they could maintain and control it while they studied what they had accidentally created.

Wiping the tears away the man quickly checked for a pulse but found none and despite the urgent need to act, stood frozen in shock, looking at the woman lying at his feet. Other than the torn lab coat, Jacob Daedalus saw no obvious signs of external injury. *Did that mean the others still didn't know what she had done? Perhaps their plan to escape could still be salvaged.*

Removing the child from the laboratory's isolation ward was an act of treason and betrayal. Everyone assigned to the program knew what the consequences would be if something like this ever happened. There would be no trial, no jury. Only a swift execution, followed by a complete disappearance of any body or evidence. A missing person's report would be filed with the proper authorities and the next of kin would be notified. The person would simply cease to exist.

How did Van even know for certain she had indeed stolen the actual P.R.I.M.E.? They had planned on testing the P.R.I.M.E. before attempting to snatch the child away from the facility. How am I supposed to do this alone? Jacob Daedalus wondered. There was a good chance she was mistaken. After all, the entire lab team had been struggling to determine a consistent way of distinguishing the P.R.I.M.E. from its replicants, with little to no success. After all, nothing like this had ever existed before. The P.R.I.M.E. was truly an anomaly.

Dr. Jacob Daedalus took in these facts and all signs pointed to trouble. Big trouble.

When things didn't go according to how he had methodically planned their escape, his normal course of action would have been to gently place the bundled child next to the dead woman, and calmly walk back to his laboratory. Maybe try again at another time when the opportunity presented itself.

He was leaning over to do that, when suddenly, the child in his arms felt twice as heavy as it had been a moment before and he nearly dropped the baby to the ground. Glancing down, the man could have sworn he counted two sets of hands and feet within the bundle.

However, when he adjusted the blanket in order to examine it more closely, it contained only the one child.

Could Van have stolen the actual P.R.I.M.E.? What am I getting myself into? He asked himself. But knowing he may not get another chance now, his legs were already moving him and the child in the direction of the stairwell leading to the parking garage. With his security clearance, unlike many of the other researchers Van included, leaving wasn't the problem. It was what came after that worried him. He hoped he could escape before security really knew what was happening. If he could get out of the facility, he should be able to reach his contacts on the outside, albeit sooner than expected. The airport was less than thirty-five minutes away. He could be on a plane within the hour. Plenty of time as long as they didn't know the P.R.I.M.E. was gone and came after him in full force.

Dr. Daedalus's answer would come soon enough. In the meantime, he honored a dead friend's request and tried to make certain the baby was safe.

— — — — —

It took Director Gray years to reclaim his P.R.I.M.E..

They came for them in the middle of the night. The unfortunate family that lived in the front unit that the boy and Dr. Daedalus were renting from were butchered and killed first. Director Gray's orders had been clear: Recover the P.R.I.M.E. and the doctor at all costs and leave no witnesses.

Dr. Jacob Daedalus had studied extensively how people had survived and hidden themselves during the Holocaust and other times in history when people were forced to hide from the state or other enemies with extremely vast resources.

Living a life of shadows, they never stayed anywhere too isolated nor too public, and never so long as to become recognizable or known to anyone. Most of Daedalus's time was spent creating elaborate new identities for them to slip into quickly should the need ever arise. He taught the boy how to keep away from situations where their true identity might be exposed, but still somehow despite all of this they had been found.

The boy had barely escaped from the home squeezing between walls and then crawling underneath the subfloor of the structure. 'Daeda', that's what the boy had taken to calling Dr. Jacob Daedalus, had made the secret escape access, as he did wherever they stayed, in case they were ever discovered.

"Wake up child. You must hurry." Daedalus whispered in the boy's ear awakening him.

The boy barely had time to put on his shoes without socks before Daedalus shoved a backpack with money and other supplies into his hands. The boy quickly slipped the pack over his shoulders before climbing into the hidden hole in the wall.

Daeda would always tell the boy the same thing when he showed him how to access whatever particular route he had devised, "If you should ever have to use this, run. Run as fast as you can." Daeda said to the boy as he chiseled out drywall and re-plumbed the pipes to allow room enough for the boy but no larger, "Don't look back. Don't go to friends or neighbors for help, because they might be compromised too. Try to escape and lose yourself the way I've taught you."

So the boy escaped. The boy had watched only briefly through a crack in the hidden wall partition, as the intruders tied Daeda down and began 'questioning' him on the whereabouts of the missing child, before climbing down between the plumbing and electrical pipes to the small crawlspace underneath the building.

The sounds of torture still echoed in the boy's head as he squeezed himself through the tight passage that would eventually lead him to an access tunnel to the sewer system and into the darkness below the city.

Once in the sewer tunnels, the boy flicked on the flashlight Daeda had supplied in the backpack. The light it created flickered across dark, dank walls, while the ceiling overhead seemed to be crumbling away. In this subterranean environment, no matter how carefully he tread, there was a danger he could lose his footing on the slippery surface, so his progress at first was slow, listening to the hushed drip of water.

That is until he heard the enormous explosion come from what he thought was his old home. The heat from the blast was coming at him and despite the danger of slipping in the dark he began running as fast as he could. The air was close and putrid, making it unpleasant and difficult to breathe as he furiously made his way through the underground labyrinth. Far off in the distance, the sound of a gushing torrent from an unseen channel could be faintly heard and so he followed that and it wasn't long before he reached a metal ladder leading up to the surface. Wanting nothing more than to be free of the black subterranean pit he began to climb.

At that time of night the streets were completely deserted, but the boy wasted no time and began sprinting down the road. Despite not even knowing from whom he was running, it was the terror of being caught that drove the boy to run faster than he ever had, before eventually falling in a heap to the ground. Crying out in pain and gasping to catch his breath he could do nothing but lay there for a time. The boy pulled his bloodied knees in and held them tucked up against his chest forming a tight fetal position.

While on the ground, the boy imagined a form of himself looking down at his own curled-up body. The duplicate briefly stood there before it ran away. Escaping.

The second time he envisioned another, more confident version of himself standing up, as if it were ready to charge back up towards the house taking on anything that might still be there. Once again, this more fearless self-image sprinted off in the direction the first one had. This mental exercise made him feel better, so the boy repeated the process over and over in his head. Each time a version of himself ran away, he wished the horrible memories and emotions would leave with it. He drove away the terrible thoughts that hurt him so badly, until his heart rate and breathing slowed down and his body relaxed.

He rose to his feet disoriented by this self-inflicted

amnesia. The horrific memories were gone but so were other vital aspects of himself.

Lost and confused, he walked in the same direction he had imagined himself going while still huddled in a ball on the ground, a short while earlier. Still burdened by a sense of grief and loss but now not knowing why, each step carried more weight than his small limbs could measure.

The boy's first night found him hidden away in the local urban sprawl. He collapsed in exhaustion behind a fast-food restaurant chain's trash bin. At that point he was so tired and hungry he didn't care anymore if he was even found or not. Hunger and discomfort outweighed his fear of capture. But the pursuers, if there ever were any, never came for him that night.

He dug into his backpack and pulled out some money to buy some food. He was cold and hungry with nowhere to go. An empty vessel lost at sea, yet not alone.

The P.R.I.M.E. was never truly alone.

CHAPTER 1
DAILY ROUTINE

Los Angeles, California

Caught in the usual morning commuter traffic, Shane Fisher stared down at the freeway's pavement watching the steam rise up towards him. The hot odor penetrated his nostrils and left an acidic taste in his mouth before he could roll up his window. Looking down at the freeway when it came to a dead stop always gave Shane an uncomfortable feeling. There was something unnatural about it, as if the lines and reflectors were only to be seen at high speeds or something. Maybe it was because it usually meant a horrific car accident had occurred and someone had died.

His car idled and hissed, threatening to overheat as he sat less than a quarter mile away from his exit. If he got out and walked the rest of the way to work, he would probably get there faster.

The early morning commute was the worst part of his workday, because driving gave Shane too much time alone with his own thoughts. With the whole world in front of him, the most Shane could say he had accomplished was working his way up from a book shelver to manager of the local Brent & Nigel's bookstore.

By the time Shane had worked a full day and driven home, what time he had left remaining usually amounted to eating, maybe drinking some cheap beer or expensive wine, reading a little, surfing the web and checking his email, before crashing out. Just to do it all over the next day. Everything else fell within the cracks of the fits and frenzies of his otherwise torpid life. Before he knew it, ten years had whisked by in this procession of banal events, peppered with the occasional emotional meltdowns and drunken episodes that he had naively mistook as genuine life experiences.

Shane felt nervous that he had done so little in so long a time.

Remember Shane, things are never so bad that they can't get a little bit worse. Shane half-jokingly reminded himself. Lately, more than ever, Shane could not shake the feeling something was missing from within him. Essential pieces of himself were left behind or lost somewhere. He felt incomplete, and thus, his life suffered and reflected the same deficient symptom.

Shane eventually arrived at work and parked his car in a strip mall, a carbon copy that can be seen in most suburbs across the entire country's landscape. He shook off the usual melancholy, which accompanied the doubt anything was ever really going to change, and gave a loud sigh, before getting out to start the workday. Shane locked his car and listened for the double beep his obsessive-compulsive behavior insisted on hearing before walking towards the side door of Brent & Nigel's bookstore.

The head cashier, Pete Schilling, was already there, both hands filled with a large coffee, waiting for Shane to open up. Pete called out, way too eager for this time in the morning, "Hey, Shane, how's it going, boss?"

"Same as always, Pete. Slightly hung-over, bitter, and ready to help people get their read on." Shane said to his exuberant coworker.

Pete always arrived to work earlier than everyone else. Pete had the odd habit of sipping from two coffees, a custom he said he had acquired while in the United States Army. Black in the left hand; a heavy dose of cream and sugar in the right hand. "Impossible to get that second cup once you get out of the chow line," Pete often remarked to nobody in particular, perhaps knowing the habit was a bit peculiar, especially given that he was no longer in the Army, but Shane never asked the old guy more about it.

"You just need that first coffee," said Pete, taking a sip from the left hand and then his right.

Shane grinned as he placed his key into the lock of the side door. Already shaking off most of the negative feelings he had built up on the freeway drive. Actually, he really did like his job. He loved books and bookstores. Loved introducing people, old and young, to the amazing worlds and insights resting between the pages.

Unfortunately, like most jobs, the pay was sufficient to survive on but never quite enough to get ahead or save anything. It's not like he made enough to get his own apartment or anything.

Now out of college, Shane still lived at home with his mother and he was nervous concerning what he was going to do next. The real problem was he had no clue what he wanted to do with the rest of his life. Like a lot of young adults his age, Shane was actually stalled out by having too many options in front of him. If somebody asked him what he wanted to study and do now, his honest answer would be 'everything'. But nobody can be good at everything or know everything. He would have to live at least a thousand lifetimes to study all of the subjects he was really interested in, which is why he suspected he always liked working at the bookstore, surrounded by all of the knowledge contained there.

Which road should I take and will it be the correct one? He often wondered to himself. Shane figured he'd let life take him and see where he ends up.

"Hi, Shane," Angelica Preston called from behind him, "OMG, why does it have to be so hot outside and so cold in this place? And I hate opening shifts."

"Hey, Angie," Shane replied without glancing back, as he pushed the door open with his shoulder while ejecting the key in a practiced fluid motion. He headed towards the alarm control next to the main double doors near the store's front entrance.

"Maybe if you wore warmer clothes–," Shane muttered the suggestion under his breath, as he punched in the ridiculous 1,2,3,4 # alarm code combination, which was the same code to every retail store he had ever worked for since he was seventeen. *I mean why bother with an alarm at that point?* Yet still, out of habit more than anything else, he covered up the keypad with his fingers.

"Huh?" Angie was following closer behind him

than he had thought.

Could she have heard me? "You're here earlier than usual," Shane sputtered, quickly changing the subject.

"Yeah, I know. Stupid Brian called me in to do the inventory with him. I was already here so late last night, doing recovery and restocking." Angie groaned with frustration, "It's not fair, Shane! Just because he has an obvious crush on me, why does he get to stick me on all of his crappy shifts?" She kept pouting, "I mean it's obvious all he really wants to do is stare at my boobs all day." Angie leaned in as if to emphasize the two guilty suspects in question.

Well, maybe if you wore warmer clothes… "Brian is the music department manager, Angie. It's his call, but I'll talk to him," Shane said, not having a clue what he would say to Brian.

"Thanks, Shane. You rock!" Angie said on her way to the back of the store where the partitioned movie and music department was located.

Shane simply nodded a response.

He liked to think of the average Brent & Nigel's bookstore as the perfect cross-section of life and society. On the one hand, you have your genuine and honest bookseller, like Pete, earnestly trying to help those few individuals left in the world who still read to find what they are looking for. On the other hand, you always find the transient, neo-literate degenerates whose only real goal is to deploy all manner of sick means at their immediate disposal to torment those decent folks with whom they work in order to pass the time more quickly.

When describing these misanthropes, Shane would often quote Hunter S. Thompson: "At best they were unreliable, and at worst they were drunk, dirty and no more dependable than goats."

If Pete, the old vet, were of the former, then Brian, the movie and music department manager, was definitely of the latter type. And Angie… well, she fell somewhere in between.

She was hired a couple of months ago, and it was no secret that pretty much every male in the store had a crush on Angelica Preston. She, in turn, had an even bigger thing for Shane. Shane was not interested, which ironically fueled Angie's fire for him even more. He couldn't put his finger on it. After all, Angie was unbelievably pretty, and Shane did find himself occasionally stealing a glance at her tall and slender form, as he caught himself doing while they clocked in at the information desk computer. Yet even so, there was something that did not quite gel.

Shane headed to the back office for his usual managerial duties to open the store. After grabbing his phone-pager, clipboard, and doing the morning's deposit and counting out the drawers for the other cashiers, Shane headed upstairs to receiving where the days delivery of books would be arriving at any moment.

On his way up the escalator, he noticed Skylar, the coffee shop manager, brewing fresh coffee and warming up the various baked goods for the cafe.

"Smells good down there Skylar!" Shane called down to her, as the rich aroma of baked pastries and java wafted around the bookstore.

"I'll have a fresh baked tray of peanut-butter cookies for samples in a minute, Shaney. You should come down here when you're done and try one." she called up to him.

"Did I mention how much you rock yet today, Sky?"

"Ha! You only love me for my sweets." She flirted.

"Oh come on, Skylar. You know I love you for more than just your cookies." Shane called back. So began the usual daily routine of a retail chain bookstore, which was the monotony of Shane's life for several years now.

Little did he know that in the next few hours, his life was going to be changed forever by circumstances that were completely out of his control.

CHAPTER 2
THE CREW

"So, I say back to the guy, 'If it don't come out of a rig or a bottle, I ain't touchin' it," said the largest man in the room.

"What's a rig?" Jeff asked.

"Fool, you know what I'm saying man, a harpoon," the big man said, gesturing to his arm, sinking the plunger of an imaginary drug syringe.

Jeff's eyes dilated in understanding. He immediately desired to leave the place, but knew it was too late. The large man, irritated at the interruption, was now focused on him.

"Who are you anyhow? I ain't never seen you here before. Damn, I hate it when Wayne uses new guys. Always messin' things up. Like you messed up my story." The big man moved in, closing the gap between himself and Jeff with a single quick stride.

"What's your name? And how the hell are you up on this gig?" asked the giant, the tattoos on his enormous arms flexing and tensing. Jeff braced for the big man to punch him in the next instant.

"Leave him alone, Manny. He's a curious kid. Finish your story before Wayne gets here." The blonde man, who had introduced himself earlier as Cole, when Jeff had first arrived, spoke from behind the giant's mountainous shoulders. "He's not hip to all your druggy lingo is all," the man chuckled.

"Screw him! Now, I forgot where I was. And, he still hasn't answered my questions." Manny returned his gaze back on Jeff.

Now the blonde guy, Cole, was between Jeff and Manny, knowing how fast Manny could lose his temper. "Cool down there, partner. You want Wayne to walk in on you ripping this poor guy's arms off? Let's cool those jets and remember how much Wayne said this job could be worth." This comment by Cole got the big man's attention quickly. Manny's hands, which were already raised and gripped tightly into enormous wrecking-balls, lowered to his sides and the veins on his face and neck immediately softened at the first mention of the money Wayne had promised.

"Ah, come on, Cole. Let's see the big guy work this kid over a little. We'll pull him off before he does too much damage. Besides, I think I've heard this story like a billion times already," said Trent, the usual instigator to Manny's reckless physical outbursts. Standing barely more than five feet tall, with rat-like and pointy facial features, Trent was the virtual opposite to Manny's large physical stature. Trent clearly derived a sadistic pleasure in the destruction caused by Manny. Trent was usually the guy who would sneak up and slit the throat of Manny's victims once Manny was finished with them.

Cole, ignoring Trent's comment, continued calming the giant, "Now, why don't you go over there and finish the rest of your story for the other guys? Let me find out what's up with this dude." Cole was already turning back towards Jeff. "You really need to learn who to interrupt. Manny hates losing his train of thought, as you can see." Cole was smiling now. "But he did have a point. You are new to this crew, and it's not like Wayne to bring in unknowns for jobs this big. What's your story, kid?"

"I work in computers and Wayne used to date my mom. She danced at the White Rhino for a little while. That's how she paid for my education. I guess that's how they met." Jeff wasn't ashamed his mom had worked as an exotic dancer in order to pay the tens of thousands in college expenses he had accrued getting his computer science degree. He intended to make it up to her and pay her back tenfold, and if the job was as big as Wayne promised, he could do it with this single job.

"So, you're the computer hacker Wayne was talking about." Cole turned back towards Manny and the others, "Good thing you didn't rip the guy's arms off. Looks like we need this guy's hands and brain to do this thing."

"Wayne seems to think you're pretty good with computers. Are you?" asked Cole, turning back towards Jeff.

"I specialize in network and firewall security. If I want inside someone's system, I'll get in," Jeff said with simple certainty.

When it came to computers, Jeff exuded confidence. Ever since he was a kid, Jeff could get computers to do whatever he wanted them to do. He wrote his first program when he was thirteen. Two years later in high school, he was hacking into his school's network to change his friends' grades; for a small fee, of course. It was the challenge Jeff really enjoyed. In college, he was responsible for crashing the main servers on three major credit card companies and causing rolling blackouts with the electrical company.

"What is more important," added Jeff, "I'm good at doing things and not getting caught. Every keystroke leaves a digital imprint, a footprint, if you will. It's how the authorities trace it. But there are ways of sending them in the wrong direction."

Cole's smile returned, "That's good, 'cause from the little details I've already heard, this job is going to require some serious brains and muscle." Cole gestured with a slight nod of his head towards Manny and the other two men in the room.

The door to the old warehouse they were in opened suddenly by a hulking bodyguard, though still not nearly as big as Manny. Wayne had arrived. The click-tap sound of Wayne's ever-present walking stick could be heard announcing the fat gangster's entrance.

"Gentlemen," Wayne spoke, before he had fully entered into the room, "let's skip the usual bullshit and get right to it, shall we? I told you all about a job with the potential to make us all very rich men. I've selected each of you for the unique talents you bring. The five of you will make up the main team with a few scattered support people."

Wayne looked at each of them before eventually coming to rest on Jeff. "Has everyone had a chance to meet my young friend here?" Wayne put his fat arm around Jeff. "Jeffrey is an absolute genius at computers.

Isn't that right, kiddo?"

Jeff nodded his head in affirmation. But before he could speak a reply, Wayne had let go of him and walked over to the fifth and only member of the assembled crew Jeff had yet to be introduced to. "And with Fragile coming out of retirement for this one last gig, we are in good shape people!"

Fragile was exactly as his namesake implied. The man looked like he was going to fall down. Half bent over from a spinal deformity, Fragile's body was completely asymmetrical. One arm looked to be half the size of the other; the smaller of the two hung limp and uselessly at his side, while his other hand shook incessantly like the man was riddled with Parkinson's disease.

Even without knowing exactly what the job entailed, Jeff wondered to himself how in anyway this 'fragile' man could be an asset. However, Jeff was quickly finding that he was completely out of his element and nothing was as it first appeared.

Fragile stood there with no indication he even cared about Wayne's compliment. The man looked like he was in pain at the effort of standing there. "Thanks, Wayne, but am I mistaken or did you not mention something about skipping the bullshit?" Fragile spoke with a soft voice, allowing him to sound erudite even while cursing.

"Right you are old friend. We are not as young as we once were and time is of the essence. After all, the job in question goes down in a little over four hours, so let's get started. Shall we?" Wayne smiled at the shocked look on the faces of these seasoned operators. The air fully sucked from it, the entire room had suddenly fallen silent. Except for Cole, whose blood was laced with ice water, the crew looked visibly fazed by this new revelation.

Fittingly, it was Cole first to speak up, raising an objection to the sudden news based on logistical concerns. "Wayne, of course, you're joking right? I mean that's not what we had planned. I thought this was our initial meet. We haven't had time to make the proper preparations necessary to–"

"No need to concern yourself with that." Wayne cut him off, holding up his hand. "I'm still waiting on the exact location of the job myself, but I expect that call to come in any minute. But relax guys, everything has been set into motion, in some cases months ago, and I can assure you every detail has been put neatly into place."

CHAPTER 3
THE JOB

"I'm really sorry, ma'am, but our corporate policy has changed. We no longer accept book returns without a receipt. Plus, even if we did, those books would have to be in 'like-new' condition." Shane patiently explained to the irate lady, holding a weather beaten and worn stack. The books in question looked as if she had found them at a swap meet or garage sale and was trying to return them for a cash profit. It was a common scam at Brent & Nigel's before the corporate office in New York wised up and changed their policy.

"These books have clearly been loved by someone, and in some cases, it looks like the household pet. Do you, by chance, own a dog or puppy?" Shane attempted to make light of the situation, but at the same time, make it clear he was in no way going to take the books off the lady's hands.

"I want to speak to your manager," demanded the lady in the floral moo-moo. "This is unbelievable! I've been coming here for over five years and have never had a problem returning books before."

Which is exactly why we changed the policy. Shane thought but said instead, "Again, I am terribly sorry, ma'am, but I am the manager on duty, and I simply cannot take these books in the condition they are in. Especially without a receipt."

"I want to speak with your superior!" The lady

was red in the face now, almost purple actually, and was clearly going to escalate things. Luckily, it was only five minutes after opening. The store was mostly empty, except for a few of the regulars who came in when the doors opened and Shane's good friend, Ray, who was busy getting his morning coffee over at the cafe. Ray was the manager of the bank located three doors down from Brent & Nigel's.

Shane had enough at this point, "Listen, here's what I can do. Do you see this bar code right here?" Shane said, looking around and leaning in conspiratorially close towards the woman, as he turned over one of the battered hard covers. "This barcode and thirteen digit number right here is called an ISBN, I'm sure you've noticed them before. Do you know what they do?"

"No" the lady replied hesitantly.

Shane smiled to himself. *Good, this will be easy then.* He spoke in the most professional voice he could muster. "What it does is track every single book that has one. It works kind of like a thumbprint and allows us to see where and when it was purchased and by whom," Shane continued, "or if the book was ever lost or stolen even," Shane put a little extra emphasis on the latter part. "So, all I would need from you is your full name, address and phone number and we can see exactly when and where you purchased these books. Of course, because of the legality issues involved your name will be processed through our central data base, but it's just a part of the process of doing a search like this and you have nothing to worry–" Shane didn't even have time to continue with the story he was making up, before the lady had scooped the pile of books from the counter and was on her way out the front doors.

"You might want to try Borderline Books," Shane called after the lady.

"Wow, what a load of crap you fed that one. I can't believe she fell for it. Even I know book barcodes don't work like that and I'm a banker, not a book nerd like you." Ray joked, as he walked up with his coffee.

"I know. She's probably going to go home and ask her nephew or something to look up ISBN barcodes on the Internet. She's going to be a nice beet-red color when she finds out." Shane was clearly pleased with his handy work. He turned to Angie, who had called him over when the lady insisted on speaking with a manager at the first refusal of the books. "And that, my young protégé, is how you scam a scammer. I will now bid you adieu. It is time for a little more caffeine." Shane bowed with a cheesy flourish, heading off towards the cafe for his second coffee of the morning with banker Ray by his side.

"Thanks for dealing with the mean chick. She was seriously agro," Angie called after him.

Shane simply gave her a thumbs-up without looking back and continued on towards the aroma of Skylar's freshly brewed coffee.

Shane glanced at his watch: 10:15am. The bookstore had been open for a little over an hour and he was ready to go home. "So, what do you have going on today, Ray?"

"Nada mucho, my friend, the same as usual. Push my tellers to open more savings accounts, count money, deal with pissed off people whose accounts are overdrawn and get charged a fee, count more money, yada yada yada. But hey, at least it's Friday, right?" Ray sighed with the deep sigh of someone who has worked a nine to five job for too long. "Plus, I'm at the branch next to your sorry ass and we can be miserable on our breaks together. And, I get free coffee from Skylar, because she thinks it might help her chances with you, if you ever decide to notice she has a serious crush on you. Besides, the stuff they call coffee over there at the bank is just plain nasty. I wouldn't–"

Shane cut him off, before they got any closer to the cafe, "Dude, maybe you should lay off the coffee? I'm going for a second cup, but you are freakishly wired today. Your mouth is moving a mile a minute. Now shut up, before Skylar hears you. I know she likes me, but I don't know exactly how or what to do next."

"Coffee is the broth of Satan," Ray joked, "And I say thank you Satan. Besides you know I'm only kidding, broski. I seriously want to–" Ray was again cut off, this time by his cell phone ringing loudly from his pocket. "Damn, it's the bank. Hold up a sec." Ray pressed the accept button and spoke professionally for the first time all morning, "This is Ray. Oh, hello sir. Yes sir, I was on my five-minute…Ur, uh, absolutely sir… Uh huh. No, I've never had to do one of those before. I'll be right there." Ray clicked the end call button and stopped dead in his tracks, turning back towards the front doors. "Gotta go, dude."

"What the hell was that all about?" Shane called after him.

"I have no idea, but my district manager is standing in the branch right now. There is some kind of big money transfer going down at the bank and he wants me over there. STAT!" Ray said over his shoulder, half sprinting now.

"Right, I'll see you at lunch. Mr. Chen's or Louie's pizza?" Shane called after him, but Ray was already out the door.

CHAPTER 4
PARTNERING UP

Jeff wore ultra lightweight body armor and it was making him sweat profusely. "I don't see why I have to wear this stuff, I'm going to be in the van the whole time anyway, aren't I?" he said to nobody in particular, unable to conceal his nervousness.

"Shut your mouth and do as you're told! Consider yourself lucky, Wayne told me that our military doesn't even have access to this kind of equipment. Poor suckers have to deal with last century gear." Trent was actually deriving pleasure from the fact that the military GIs had to make do with the old heavy and cumbersome Kevlar equipment. Meanwhile, private contractors, if their pockets were deep enough, had access to all kinds of advanced body armor and weapons usually utilized during covert black-ops missions. These kind of military operations invoked phrases like 'plausible deniability' and 'acceptable collateral damage'.

"This whole job sucks," Manny was not happy. "Never had to wear this kinda stuff before," he grumbled.

"Relax, big fella. Be grateful they made some gear that actually fits you," Trent reassured his exceedingly large friend.

"I guess we're lucky they made them kids sizes for you too then," added Manny, obviously angry at his small friend's attempt at making light of the unusual situation. Manny did not like deviations from the norm, and this was definitely not the norm.

"Screw you, Emmanuel. Let's see the next time I try to cheer your sorry ass up." Trent only called Manny by his given name when he was irritated or nervous. The hastiness of the situation was placing everyone a little bit on edge.

Never before had any one of them been asked to perform a job within hours of finding out what it actually was. This didn't leave a whole lot of time for planning and preparation. Nevertheless, Wayne had assured them everything down to the smallest detail had been carefully thought through. Plus, the money, once the actual dollar amount was disclosed, made it difficult for any of them to turn down.

"Can you both please shut up and finish getting geared up? You guys sound like a couple of whining babies." Cole said, silencing them. Cole was dealing with the situation in his typical professional and calculating manner, a reflex for him when he was nervous. "Wayne wants us ready in the next thirty minutes. You all heard what he said, the success of this job depends on the timing, and we are not going to fail. I don't know about you idiots, but now that I know exactly how much we can make on this thing, I'm willing to wear a chicken suit if I have to in order to get the job done."

"If I may suggest another way of looking at the situation," Fragile was leaning his weak body against the far wall of the small room they were all in taking a drag off of his cigarette. Fragile wasn't required to wear the body armor for his role in the operation, but he was still waiting in the back of the warehouse with the rest of the crew.

Fragile flicked ash from the cigarette he was smoking with his one good hand. "The body armor represents the seriousness of this job and what is at stake for all of us should we blunder any single aspect of it." Fragile took another slow deep hit from his cigarette before continuing, "If you men care for my advice, I would take the next few minutes before we embark on this excursion and reduce your thoughts to solely the task at hand and perhaps leave your usual arrogant bluster in this room." When he said this last part, Fragile stared directly at Trent and Manny.

"What did the cripple just say? I can't never understand a single word the guy says sometimes." Manny was already on his feet slamming ammo-filled magazines into the slide casings of the vast array of weapons he was concealing on various places of his body.

"He said you should shut up, concentrate on your job and everything will go fine today. There is no reason to be nervous." Trent was also sliding small guns and, of course, knives, his silent and up close weapon of choice, into the various pockets of his clothing. "Let's not forget, this ain't our first rodeo and, with the exception of the techie kid, we're all professionals here." Trent spoke to Manny but was really addressing the entire room.

"I want you to put all of your personal belongings into those lockers over there." Cole addressed the assembled men, as he gestured to a row of old lockers in the far corner of the room. "Anything and everything that can identify you, including your wallet, car keys and mobile phone. Your stuff will be here when we meet back afterwards, and if anything goes wrong, nothing should be able to track back to any of us," Cole reminded the group.

Jeff walked over to where Cole and Fragile were standing together, "I have to take my laptop with me. It isn't identifiable to me in any way and I have a couple of really cool programs on it, just in case it were ever to get lost or stolen."

"Like what?" Fragile asked politely, not really interested but could tell Jeff wanted to discuss it.

"Well, for instance, I can erase the entire hard drive as well as GPS track the laptop from anywhere using a unique program that I wrote for it." Jeff bragged to the old man, as they both put their personal belongings into the storage lockers.

"Is that something you have ever needed to do before?" Fragile asked.

"No, but as a hacker, you never know when it may come in handy to erase everything remotely in case the cops get a hold of it. Or, if it ever gets stolen, I can track them down and get my hardware back." Jeff said with a bit too much bravado. He was trying to play the role of a hardened criminal. Fragile could tell the kid was naive and kind of enamored with the whole tough guy image. For Fragile, that was always a more unfortunate side effect of doing this kind of business.

After a few more minutes, the group was assembled and readying to exit the room.

"Fragile, hold up a second. I need to go over one last detail of the plan with you." Cole said, as the others left the room.

"Of course, Cole." Fragile remained behind, leaving Cole and the older man alone.

Cole waited till he was certain the others were out of ear shot before saying, "After the money-bags are placed into the van, you and I are going to have less than fifteen minutes alone with them before we get back here. While I am driving I need you to check and make sure one of those bags contains a sealed envelope. As you know, that sealed envelope is more important than anything else. The money can burn for all I care." Cole's eyes burned with intensity as he said this, "Do you understand what I'm telling you, Fragile? For us, what's inside that envelope is the job. The money, as far as you and I are concerned, is merely... a distraction. It was a way to manipulate Wayne into doing this gig and a means to transport the contents of that envelope safely."

"I understand, Cole. Don't forget this was my plan to begin with. I will retrieve the envelope before any of the others have a chance to." Fragile would do his job, like he always did, with little talk and perfect execution.

The two men left the small cramped room and assembled themselves with the others in the much larger abandoned parking garage of their safe house. Parked there waiting for them were two white work vans, and a nondescript blue sedan.

"Ok, everyone, let's go over it one more time." Cole explained the plan of action in detail, one last time before the drive.

"It's going to consist of six phases, with each phase being timed, coordinated and initiated by me." Cole reiterated for the third time since Wayne had left. "In Phase One, Jeff will take control of all electronics, cameras, and computers in the bank."

"That's so simple it's almost laughable. I wish I had a real challenge." Jeff interrupted.

"Phase Two," Cole continued, ignoring Jeff's exuberance. "Fragile, you will enter the bank and engage the manager and get him to take you to the back near the safety deposit boxes and vault."

Fragile simply nodded a confirmation that he understood what his role would entail.

"Phase Three, will begin precisely when Fragile and the bank manager go to the back. Trent, you and Manny will restrain any security and take physical control of the bank, locking it down. Nobody comes in and nobody leaves. Trent will go to the back and subdue the distracted bank manager and take the vault key from him. If the bank manager refuses to cooperate, Fragile is to be used as a decoy. Trent will pretend to threaten Fragile's life, causing Fragile to begin feigning a heart attack. That ought to get the manager to comply. No bank manager is going to let a customer die over federally insured money. Trent? Manny? You got all that?" Cole asked.

"Yeah, yeah. This job is almost stupid easy," was

Trent's only comment.

"Good, I'm glad you think so, because this is where it gets a bit more complicated." Cole explained, "Phase Four is cracking the bank's vault. This particular bank vault has a three tier locking system. The first obstacle is a computer program, which sends a signal to the police if the power were ever to be cut to the vault or bank. Jeff's first task will be to circumvent this signal and block it. Next, the power to the vault's lock has to be cut, rendering it a purely mechanical locking mechanism. You guys with me so far?" Cole asked, waiting for an affirmative response from each of the crew members before continuing.

"Good, now, this is where the manager's key comes into play. Along with the key, a combination will need to be provided in order to gain access. The combination is on a timing system, which allows the manager on duty access to a randomly chosen new combination every half hour. Trent, you will have to connect a small laptop to the vault's lock and allow Jeff to run a specific program, sort of like an auto-dialer, that will run through approximately twenty-one thousand combinations every fifteen seconds." Cole needed the crew to not screw this part up, because, despite Jeff's control of the power system, they had precisely a minute before an off-sight backup system kicked in. On trial runs with a similar vault locking system, security companies have shown that the process usually took under two minutes. Jeff was convinced he could do it in the sixty-seconds while the power was out.

Cole continued, "Trent will then open the bank

vault. Phase Five: While Trent and Manny are preparing the money for transport, I will leave my place in the van and move the white van from behind the building to the front of the building and enter the bank. Finally, Phase Six: I will enter the bank and will load the money into the van and drive back with Fragile to the safe house. Trent and Manny will leave in Fragile's blue sedan parked in the front. Jeff will drive the communications van. Now, I want everybody to confirm that they understand every detail I have just explained." Everyone groaned an acknowledgment not wanting to go over it yet again.

This was the plan and Cole explained everyone's role with the cool efficiency more akin to a military squad leader than a gangster. Unless he gave explicit orders to do so, no one was to deviate from the plan. This really meant no killing, with extra emphasis directed at Trent and Manny.

"We got it, Cole. No killing." Trent said, "It sounds to me you've gone over every detail so methodically. I see no reason anything should come to that." Trent said sarcastically, as he gave Manny a big wink.

"Okay, if nobody has any questions then let's get moving. Fragile, you're in the sedan. Trent, you and Manny are in that van over there, and Jeff will ride with me in the other one." Cole was assuming his usual leadership role now.

Jeff couldn't help but notice, despite his confidence, how young Cole was. He couldn't be much older than Jeff, yet Cole acted like he had been doing this kind of thing as long as Fragile had. Plus, with the blonde hair and constant smile he looked more like the guy you would go see a movie or pick up on girls with rather than a ruthless criminal.

"Hey Jeff, quit daydreaming and get in the van already. We gotta go." Cole was already sliding behind the wheel and turning the key to the ignition.

As he got into the passenger seat next to Cole, Jeff glanced into the back of the van.

"Whoa, look at all this gear… oh my god, wow! Is that a parallel design NVIDIA, super-cluster micro-processor?" Jeff thought he had died and gone to computer nerd heaven. The van was to act as Jeff's domain during the operation as well as a command post for Cole to direct the operation initially, until it was time for him to leave the van and get his own hands dirty. What Jeff saw defied all logical sense to him. The shear amount of computer gear, communications equipment and technology that was packed into the back was probably worth a small fortune by itself.

The equipment was so advanced and profoundly expensive something in Jeff's sharp mind couldn't help but wonder if there was more to the job than what Wayne had let on to earlier.

Cole interrupted the young man's reverie abruptly, "Put your nerd boner back in your pants and buckle up. We can't be pulled over by some cop for a seat-belt ticket right now. You'll have plenty of time to play with all the toys back there once we are in place and the other guys are setting themselves up."

Wayne had been right regarding Jeff's talent. He was smart and knew his stuff. Cole saw how the hacker had barely glanced in the back of the van and was identifying equipment most computer experts didn't even know existed yet. Cole read into the look on Jeff's face after seeing the equipment. Between the body armor and all of the gear in this van, Jeff was doing the mental math.

If only you saw what was inside the other van. Cole thought to himself. There was everything except for a tank in the back of the van Trent and Manny were now climbing into. Cole knew the two killers would not question the gear in their vehicle. Trent and Manny would see it as more toys to inflict their pain and destruction in case things got ugly on the road.

Wayne had selected a perfect team for this kind of operation. They would perform their roles with minimal questions. Cole had played his part perfectly, acting nervous enough with Wayne and the others in the dressing room to make it appear he too was as unsure of the unusual circumstances surrounding the job.

He hoped Fragile was up for this. Fragile was still as sharp as ever, but Cole had noticed that lately the old man's health had really started to decline.

Despite their careful planning, Cole feared Wayne suspected there was something more going on. The fat gangster had been in the game for far too long not to suspect something. Cole had warned Fragile days earlier that Wayne might not like the sudden news of learning the details to the job and the fact that it was going down all in the same day.

"It might cause Wayne to bailout and he's a critical piece. The last duplicate I found told me that the information we need would be transported with the money in an unmarked envelope. The money will act as a shield and cover for what is inside that envelope. We need Wayne's information network and his vast contacts within the banks, if we are going to pull this off." Cole reminded the old man. "But how the hell am I going to bring Wayne this information and make him think it was his idea? And what if Director Gray hears about Wayne poking his nose into one of his transfers? Wayne would be dead before he even knew what he was getting himself involved in."

"Relax, Cole, my boy," replied Fragile, "remember who you're talking to. I found you all of those years ago after that bastard Wayne had really done a number on you. He had you convinced that you were nothing more than a soulless killer." The old man placed his one good arm around Cole's shoulders, as he had done many times in the past. "Trust this old bugger when I say I have good information that tells me that with this kind of money, even if he wanted to, Wayne would not back out of this one. No matter what. Plus, if anybody can gather information about something big like this without being traced it's Wayne." Fragile said to Cole, as always the old guy had a plan in mind, "Mention that you heard about a large money transfer going down along with the numbers that are involved, and Wayne will do the rest. Black market information is what he deals in and he's damn good at it. We'll get that envelope, Cole."

Cole had watched Wayne very carefully from the moment he came into the safe house and explained the job to the group. Cole observed how Wayne had subtly shifted his weight from one foot to the other when he dropped the news that the job would be going down in the next few hours. He was definitely nervous about it, and it was important that Cole appeared equally anxious. As long as Cole and Fragile played their respective roles, things should go down smoothly. Cole would hate to have to put a bullet in the fat arrogant gangster.

Wayne had been a good source of both revenue and information for Cole and Fragile in the past. Without Wayne ever knowing it, Cole had used the various assignments and jobs over the years to amass a small fortune and find himself, one could say. The money from today, along with the vital information contained within that envelope, should be enough for him and Fragile to finish what they had begun so many years ago.

"I hope you're up for this one, you old bird," Cole spoke to himself, as he stole a glance back in the rear-view mirror and watched Fragile slowly make his way into the sedan.

Fragile moved with deliberate care getting into the car. His aching joints were bothering him as he carefully fastened his seatbelt and loosened and tightened his broken shaking hands on the steering wheel. Fragile glanced at the digital clock on the dashboard then crosschecked it with his digital wristwatch to make sure they were in sync 10:45am. Fifteen minutes. The clocks in all three vehicles would be meticulously set and matched by Cole. The man missed nothing. He was as cold and calculating as when Fragile had first found him years ago.

Fragile felt uneasy, despite Cole's reassurance, but he could not put his finger on what it was exactly. Something about this job didn't seem right, especially after Cole told him that they would have to be working with delinquents like Trent and Manny. Fragile and Cole always worked alone, but Cole kept saying this one was getting them too close to their real goal.

They needed it to look like a big heist, which would be both messy and complicated. Who better then Trent and Manny, the two psychopaths notorious for creating bloodbaths out of the simplest of jobs, to make things messy and complicated?

What have you gotten yourself into, you desperate old man? Fragile let out a deep exhale, before fishing a cigarette out of the breast pocket of his tweed jacket. He lit it with his old Zippo lighter and took a long slow drag. *The only problem with cigarettes is that they take too long to kill you.* Fragile joked, allowing himself a couple of last idle thoughts like this, before his brain kicked into work mode.

Fragile found himself returning to the peculiar circumstances now surrounding the job. He would review them from the beginning, trying to piece together what was really going on. He had nothing better to do as he waited for the clock to read 11:00am.

— — — — —

Ray Campbell was grateful to be sitting in a chair. He was sure he would have fallen down after hearing how much money was currently inside the bank's vault.

Seated in front of him in Ray's chair, Mr. Thomas, the bank's district manager, was going over a procedure Ray had never heard of before, let alone been asked to perform. The bank's security protocols for dealing with extremely large vault cash deposits and transfers were intense.

Ray knew the vault cash was what the bank kept for normal daily transactions, such as check cashing and cash withdrawals. Ordinarily, banks only keep enough cash on hand to meet their customer's demands for withdrawals in a business week, which is considered part of a bank's obligation to the Federal Reserve Bank. Today was not one of those days.

On this morning, Mr. Thomas was explaining to Ray, two extremely large transfers were flowing through this branch before they made their way to the armored car and security depot. One had already been dropped off while Ray was getting his coffee at Brent and Nigel's at 10:15am. The second was due in the next few minutes at 11am.

"The armored car company will be here at 12:30pm." Mr. Thomas explained. "So, we will only have to hold all of the cash for a little over an hour."

"How much total? I mean after the second delivery is made." Ray asked his boss.

"Twenty-two million. We already have nine in the cash vault right now. The remaining thirteen million will be the eleven o'clock delivery." Mr. Thomas said, in an oddly matter-of-fact way, as if he were describing what he was planning to eat for lunch.

Ray whistled at the amount. He had dealt with a couple million flowing through his branch before, especially on a weekend during the holiday-season, but never anything quite like this before.

All that cash! What does it even look like? Ray thought to himself. This was new and big and, quite frankly, it made Ray nervous. Really nervous.

"Now, get out there and make sure this thing goes smoothly. Or, do you want to run over to the bookstore for another cup of coffee?" Mr. Thomas taunted, signaling their little meeting was now over. He held up a single key on a chain that Ray reverently received and placed around his own neck.

"No, sir, I'm sorry about that, sir. I mean, I would never have left the branch had I known this was all happening today." Ray sputtered getting to his feet.

"For security reasons, nobody at the branch level is ever told the specific location of a transfer ahead of time. I myself did not know the location until an hour ago. I only knew that the transfer was happening today at noon and for how much." Mr. Thomas added, "Just run your branch like normal, Campbell, and everything will be fine."

Ray nodded his head in response and walked out of his own office. Leaving his boss at his desk, Ray made his way towards the teller line to see if any of his staff needed anything. He had to force himself not to glance towards the vault behind him.

All that cash. He repeated to himself for the second time that day.

CHAPTER 5
SHANE'S LAST TASTE OF THE MUNDANE

"Have I mentioned to you lately that I hate you?" Shane said to his receiving manager as he looked at all of the day's new books that had to somehow make their way onto the sales floor. "How the hell am I supposed to get all of these books out there? You do realize I'm dealing with a finite amount of floor space, right?" Shane asked, not really expecting a response.

"Not my job and not my problem. I just zap 'em and stick 'em," Mike, the receiving manager, responded.

Mike was referring to the system of receiving and processing the store inventory's virtual mountain of books that arrived daily: scanning them into the inventory, putting the proper sticker pricing on them then placing them on carts to go out to the sales floor.

"They're your problem once I get them into the system. Now, can you please get these carts out of here? I'm expecting another delivery any minute," and with that, Mike turned his back on Shane and went back to opening boxes and unloading more books.

At major retail bookstores, books arrive every day and not only the few that are ordered for customers and the ones to refill basic inventory. Known as 'bargain' or 'discount' books these books are automatically ordered by corporate executives in a pre-negotiated deal with the various publishers and distributors, the volume of which is determined by the size and sales of the particular store. Like the hydra from mythology, it is a monster that keeps growing heads, even as the booksellers try to make gains to stop it. The more bargain books you sell, the more that arrive.

So, in his naïveté, the first few months of working at Brent and Nigel's, Shane had convinced himself that he could catch up with the endless influx of books by selling more of them. Loading customers up with stacks of books, he quickly learned he was his own worst enemy. The more books Shane sold, the more that got automatically reordered, with some titles even doubling. He tried to accept the fact that the daily job of a bookseller was to feel and, in some cases, physically and literally be buried under books.

"This is my life. I guess it's a good thing I'd rather die of exhaustion than boredom." Shane grumbled to himself, as he grabbed the handle to the nearest cart full of books and headed towards the door to the sales floor. But, before he could even reach for the handle, it burst open, slamming into a cart full of books that had been wedged too closely to the door, sending a couple of paper backs to the floor.

"I hate that slime-ball and I'm not working next to him anymore!" Angie exclaimed, stepping backwards into the room and talking to someone following behind her. It was Pete.

"What's going on, you guys? And can we please keep the screaming and cursing down to a minimum while on the sales floor?" Shane asked, as the two made their way into the receiving room.

"It's that sleazy jerk, Brian." Angie replied, "Shane, you know how small and cramped it is behind the music department counter, right? Well, he keeps using it as an excuse to rub himself on me. I mean gross!" Angelica cringed to emphasize her distaste for the music department manager. "Pete saw it, when he was back there showing a customer something. Tell him, Pete, please!" Angelica pleaded to the older head-cashier.

Shane turned to Pete for confirmation.

"I'm not saying Brian groped her or anything like that. But the guy definitely goes out of his way to break her bubble and grab extended glances." Pete said, standing erect with his hands at his sides, like he was still a soldier at attention reporting suspicious activity to a superior officer.

"Ok, ok, you guys. I'll deal with Brian right now." Shane was really getting sick of this issue with Brian and Angelica. Plus, the last thing he needed were the makings of a good old-fashioned sexual harassment lawsuit on his hands. It was time to nip this whole Brian issue in the bud once and for all.

"Angie, you are now on the book floor for the rest of the shift. Grab this cart and unload it. When you're finished with this one, Mike's got a dozen more for you after that. So you'll be spending most of your time in receiving today." Shane pushed the cart he had been wheeling out for himself towards Angelica.

She held out a single limp hand reluctantly, "Can't I work the info desk with Pete?" She asked, but Shane silenced her with a look that said: complain and

I'm shipping your ass back down to the video/music department with Brian.

"Pete, can you go down to the cafe and tell Skylar I need one of her people to cover music for me?" he asked Pete.

"Of course. I'm on it." Pete was already pulling his phone from his belt.

Shane glanced one last time at the carts filled with books piling up in the receiving room, knowing even more were coming. *I guess these will have to wait till after lunch.* Shane told himself as he went through the door to confront Brian.

While walking to the music department, Shane tried to think of the least confrontational way to tell Brian to stop being an inappropriate bastard to his co-workers. But after ruling out the first couple of ideas that had come to mind, Shane found himself already standing in the music department.

He immediately saw Brian sitting on the counter, a company policy no-no, flirting with a young female customer, trying to buy a movie. Brian had a muscular build, an attribute he liked to show off by wearing shirts that Shane thought looked two sizes too small for him.

"So, you like that actor, huh? That's cool. Actually, I think there's a new movie with him playing in the theaters right now. We should go see it together…" Shane overheard Brian hitting on the girl. Her expression showed a desire to buy her movie and leave.

"Hey, Brian, can I talk to you for a minute after you are finished helping that customer?" Shane said, maybe a little too timidly.

"I'm helping someone. Can't you see that?" Brian replied with obvious superiority.

The girl, however, used this opportunity to grab her bag and exit the department as fast as she could without actually running.

"Now, look at what you did. That chick was about to give me her digits." Brian said, apparently oblivious to the reality of the situation.

"Brian, look. I, uh, I have Angie working–" Shane said.

Brian cut him off, "Angie, yeah, where did she go? I have a ton of inventory still left for her to do in here." Brian looked around, as if for the first time, noticing Angie was gone.

Shane again attempted to speak, "Yeah, regarding that. You see, she feels uncomfortable working with you and I can't have any reports going back to corporate–"

"What did that little whore say?" Brian again interrupted Shane.

Brian threw his leg off the counter at this point and drew himself up tall, walking up close to Shane. A bit too close. An obvious intimidation tactic, but so far, it always worked on Shane. He didn't like confrontation and usually would smile and walk away from situations that even looked like they were going to get heated.

"You know, I am sick of that chick saying crap about me! She thinks she's so freaking hot and too good for anyone." Brian declared, spitting the words at

Shane.

No. Just you actually. Shane thought to himself but instead said, "Regardless, she will be working up in receiving for the rest of the day." Shane added, "and, because this is not the first time we've had a complaint, I'm going to be scheduling her for the book-floor from now on, instead of the music department. I think–"

"Dude, it'll be a total 'Sausage-Fest' back here again, if Angie leaves." Brian said. "You better not change a damn thing about her schedule. I mean it. You really don't want to get on my bad side, Fisher," Brian moved in even closer to Shane, patronizing him by using only his last name. "I've been here longer than you and I can make your life a living hell back here with 'Loss-Prevention' and other issues." Brian threatened Shane, referring to movies and music suddenly going missing, a major headache for all Brent & Nigel managers.

"She's working up in receiving for today. We can discuss it at the Manager meeting tomorrow morning," Shane said, backing down as he usually did with Brian.

"Well, that went well." Shane told himself, as he retreated from the music department and headed to receiving to tackle the incoming books before his lunch break at noon. Less than fifteen minutes away.

CHAPTER 6
WHEN TWO WORLDS COLLIDE

Jeff was in heaven. His fingers were gliding over the keyboard, as if in their natural state.

Cole had barely put the van in park at the far corner of the strip mall parking lot, before Jeff had unbuckled his seatbelt, leapt into the back and turned on all the gear.

"Take it easy, kid. We've got plenty of time for you to get comfortable with all the gear." Cole said as he glanced at the dashboard clock. 11:45am. They were exactly on time.

"Hey, trust me. I'm already comfortable. I want to run a preliminary diagnostic check on all the gear, you know, to make sure there are no software updates or anything like that." Jeff said over his machine-gun typing. "Plus, I want to take a crack at something real quick that I always like to try. It'll give me a chance to kinda test this baby out and see what she can do." Jeff added, as he hacked into several high security firewall systems faster than he had ever done before in his life.

"Just make sure you look over that red three-ring-binder. It has all the pertinent information for what it is we need you to do. Timing is critical to this going down smoothly. I don't want you punching in late, because you were too busy downloading free music or looking at porn." Cole joked.

Over the course of the drive, he had a chance to

talk to Jeff, and Cole was beginning to really like the smart young computer whiz. He reminded Cole a lot of himself at a younger age. Reasonably innocent and still optimistic.

Jeff, for his part, had already disabled and taken over control of the bank's camera, computer and power networks, including the backup generators and redundancy security systems located inside the bank itself. After a few minutes, Jeff gave Cole a thumbs up, indicating the green light signal for the rest of the team to initiate the next phase.

"Cameras are now on a constant loop. Computers are now offline, and all of the power, including the backup generator feed, is ours. The bank, for all intents and purposes, is blind, deaf and mute. The only thing not under our current control are the people inside," Jeff confirmed.

Phase One was complete. Cole gave the signal for Phase Two to commence with a single squawk through the two-way radio.

Cole, looking across the parking lot, could already see Fragile stepping out of his blue sedan slowly making his way towards the bank's entrance. He was conveniently parked in the handicapped spot directly in front of the bank. The old man was perfect. His physical appearance worked well as a distraction. It wasn't so much Fragile's body itself, as it was his movement. The movement and body mechanics were what always caught people's eye. Something about it was all wrong. As if you filmed the man then watched the video played backwards was the only way Cole could describe it.

Cole switched on the tiny microphone and earpiece each of them was wearing and asked Fragile for a confirmation the gear was working correctly. They had already run tests on this gear on the drive down the freeway, but Cole liked to double and triple check. Murphy's law was a regular stowaway on these kinds of jobs.

Fragile responded with a subtle tip of his fedora and clearing of his throat, the agreed upon signal that he could indeed hear Cole, before proceeding through the doors and disappearing into the bank.

Cole, on the other end, heard the quiet cough perfectly, as well as the image broadcasting from the micro-camera they had concealed within Fragile's hat. Fragile also carried in his jacket pocket a portable handheld cell phone jammer, which will block all mobile phones within a thousand foot range and all bandwidths from 800MHz to 1900MHz. The team's own radios, however, were set on Channel 1 at 26.965MHz, so communication between each other would not be disrupted.

"Ok, people, we've got eyes and ears now in the target zone," Cole addressed the rest of the team. "Trent, are you and Manny ready?"

"What do you think—we're jerking off here?" was Trent's reply.

"God, that guy is such a dick. What's his problem?" Jeff asked Cole making sure his own microphone was turned off before doing so.

"Ever hear of a Napoleon complex?" Cole answered, not bothering to turn his own microphone off.

"You know I can hear you, assholes?" Trent yelled over the radio system.

Everyone on the team laughed at this, even Fragile, who was already in the bank, couldn't help but smile to himself at the little sadist's anger.

After a couple of minutes, Trent and Manny could be seen coming from behind the shopping complex. They had parked the white van in the back loading area as planned and were walking around to the front. The time was exactly 12:00pm.

- - - - -

At that precise moment, Shane was exiting through the double front doors of Brent & Nigel's on his way to meet Ray at the bank for lunch. He had his phone to his ear checking his voicemail. His mom had left him a message.

"…so, anyway, I'm rambling and you must be at work already, but I really wanted to tell you about the–" but Shane never heard what followed, before his phone abruptly gave a loud screech, and the call went dead. As he was looking down at his phone wondering what could be wrong with it, Shane nearly bumped directly into one of the largest human beings he had ever seen walking into the bank.

"Excuse me. Sorry, I wasn't looking where I was going," Shane apologized.

"Stupid idiot," was all the big man said, without even bothering to turn around.

If Manny had glanced behind him, he would have been shocked to see a man who could easily have passed for the twin brother of someone he already knew. That someone was sitting in a van less than five hundred feet away.

Cole.

CHAPTER 7
ALL HELL BREAKS LOOSE

"I'm not quite sure I understand exactly what it is you would like us to do for you today, Mr.– uh, I beg your pardon, what was your name again sir?" Ray asked the crippled old man in the battered tweed suit.

Fragile ignored the man's request for a name and said, "I'll state my wishes again then. I wish to withdraw all of my funds and close my account. I would then like to place those funds in one of your safety-deposit boxes. But first I'd like you to show me the boxes so I may choose the best size suited for my purposes." Fragile patiently repeated to the young banker.

"But, sir, you understand, if it's a matter of security, your money is perfectly safe in the account it is currently in. The funds are insured by the FDIC and backed by the full faith and credit of the United States government." Ray recited the monologue every banker knew by heart.

Fragile interrupted him, "which is exactly why I want to withdraw my funds now. I've lost faith with this government's monetary system. I've spoken to my wife about the matter and we're thinking of investing in gold. Now, if you will, my young chap, I am old and my time left on this earth is limited, so may we please proceed with my desired request?"

"Of course, of course, sir," Ray had a lot of elderly folks closing their bank accounts lately. The current economy had driven them to resorting to keeping their money under the mattress again. "Let me get one of my bankers started on the paperwork for closing out the account. I'll need your full name on the account, social security number and–"

"I would very much like to see your safety deposit boxes first. I want to see what you have available and may still decide to take my funds to another bank." Fragile interrupted again. Smoothly avoiding Ray's second attempt to get the old man's personal information.

"No problem at all sir. Then if you would follow me, we'll go choose a safety-deposit box for you in the back first," Ray said.

The second enormous cash delivery had arrived a few minutes earlier. Ray's mind could only focus on getting that money out of his bank as quickly as possible. He was so distracted by this, that the old man's request hardly seemed unusual at all.

This was the part of the plan that would take Fragile to the back of the bank near the vault. Exactly where Fragile needed to be when Cole gave the green light for the next phase of the operation to begin.

"Fabulous. Let's make the journey together. Lead the way, young man." Fragile replied, slowly getting to his feet.

As the two men were heading towards the back behind the teller line, Ray couldn't help but notice an odd sight out of the corner of his eye. Coming through the doors passing the security guard at the entrance was a dwarfish little man followed by a giant.

The circus must be in town. Ray joked to himself.

The giant stopped at the desk near the front doors preparing to fill out a deposit slip or something, while the small man made his way to one of the personal banking desks at the far end of the floor.

"Hey, Ray, you ready for some lunch, bro?" He heard Shane's familiar voice call over to him.

"Not sure I'm going to be able to leave today, but wait a minute, and I'll give you some cash to bring me a pizza or something," Ray said, as he led an elderly man in an old fashion fedora and tweed coat towards the back of the bank.

"No worries. Take your time bro," Shane said, standing by an empty teller window, his usual place when he waited for Ray.

Fragile, who was following behind Ray, stopped dead in his tracks when he saw Shane.

It must be Cole. But why would he deviate from the plan? Fragile asked himself. The physical appearance and voice were Cole, however, the mannerisms were all wrong. Where Cole held himself with a confidence that exuded the swagger of a leader and ex-military man, this young man was more bookish, like a graduate student or young associate professor. Still, the similarities were remarkable, too remarkable.

Impossible, how could this be? Could the Director have found us after all of this time? Fragile thought to himself trying to dismiss that terrible possibility.

Fragile made sure to hold still long enough for the hidden camera in his hat to capture exactly what he was seeing, before hurrying to catch up with the bank manager.

Having dismissed the other more unlikely possibilities, Fragile told himself that it must be Cole playing a role that he had not told the rest of the team anything about. *But that didn't make any sense. Why would Cole expose himself to one of the bank employees?* Fragile had to force himself to dismiss this train of thought. He was now alone with the manager who held the key to the vault around his neck, and he had a job to do.

— — — — —

"Holy crap! Dude, am I seeing double, or is that guy your twin brother?" Jeff asked Cole, while they sat in the van a few hundred yards away.

Jeff rewound the recording and stopped it on the image he had just seen. He stared at the monitor then back at Cole, who was sitting right next to him, before again turning back to the duplicate image of the person on the screen.

Cole did not respond to the computer hacker's question. Instead, Cole sat quietly analyzing the bizarre situation, never taking his eyes off the monitor image.

Jeff assumed Cole must be in some sort of shock, and he didn't blame him. After all, what were the odds you would ever encounter someone who looks identical to you? One in a billion? One in several billion, perhaps? Jeff had to fight off the urge to do a couple of internet searches and write an algorithm in order to calculate the probability factors given the right phenotype, replicators, etc. But Jeff knew he had a big job to do right then, and instead hit a button allowing the live feed from Fragile's camera to return to the current time. Fragile was now in the safety-deposit box room with the bank manager, Ray.

"Fragile's in position. He's in the back room with the bank manager. Do you want me to cut the power now?" Jeff asked, without turning away from the various monitor and computer screens. When no response came, he swiveled around in his chair, "Cole?" Jeff asked, but he now found himself completely alone in the van.

— — — — —

What is going on? And, why is Cole dressed like that? Trent thought, getting nervous.

The plan was as soon as the cripple was out of sight with the manager, the lights would go dark, briefly disorienting everyone and signaling that he and Manny were to start their respective roles in this. But, Cole was simply standing there not paying attention to much of anything, looking like an idiot.

And, what the hell? Was Cole actually talking to the manager about lunch? Trent glanced over at Manny with a raised eyebrow, he too noticed, whom he thought to be Cole's unexpected deviation to the plan.

Screw it. We don't need any lights to flicker to catch anybody by surprise. Trent decided. He nodded, signaling Manny, they were to go ahead as planned, lights or no lights.

Manny nodded slightly in return and abruptly turned towards the single guard, still standing near the front door entrance. Moving with speed that was unexpected coming from a person of his size, Manny was on top of the surprised security guard in an instant. Manny snapped the unsuspecting guard's neck, under a single crushing blow to the head. He then quickly took the dead guard's keys and proceeded to lock the front doors. Nobody was getting in or out.

At the same instant, Trent turned towards the nearest teller, a hipster in his early twenties who, still unaware of what was happening, was all smiles and sunny disposition. That is, of course, until the cheery bank teller saw Trent smile back. Trent had taken out an automatic handgun with a long silencer and pistol-whipped the teller across the face.

As the unconscious teller's body fell to the floor, Trent jumped up on top of the teller line counter so he could be seen and heard by the rest of the bank's patrons and staff. "Get your stupid faces to the floor with your hands behind your back, or you're all dead," Trent screamed instructions to the bank customers, who had the unfortunate luck of deciding to cash their Friday paychecks early that day.

Trent almost casually walked over towards a middle-aged teller, who was pointlessly attempting to sound the silent alarm with the panic button hidden under her teller booth.

Standing above her, Trent kneeled down asked, "Are you having fun, yet? You really think we wouldn't think of that?" before he callously placed a bullet in the lady's head without waiting for a response. For good measure, he also shot the nearest teller, a young eighteen-year-old girl, who had been hired a week prior, making sure he had the attention of his now captive audience. Their lifeless bodies made more noise hitting the ground then Trent's silenced handgun had when turning them into corpses.

"So, who else wants to be a hero today? Anybody? Because I guarantee you will be seriously disappointed with how it turns out for you." Trent warned the remaining hostages in his nasally voice.

To hell with Cole and his no killing rule. He broke the plan first anyway by showing up early. Trent thought to himself without glancing in Shane's direction.

Trent moved towards the back, where the vault and safety-deposit rooms were located, leaving Manny and who he thought was Cole to guard the frightened and prone crowd.

— — — — —

Shane had often wondered what he would do in extreme situations, like car accidents or muggings. Always visualizing he would be heroic and brave, taking charge of the situation in a calm and controlled manner.

In reality however, Shane was frozen with terror. He could neither move nor react. If Trent and Manny hadn't mistaken him for Cole, one of them would have probably shot him dead for standing there like a fool.

"What are you doing here already?" Manny

asked, completely convinced Shane was Cole.

"I– I'm not– I was just…" Shane stammered out a nonsensical response.

Manny didn't know quite what to think of this. Luckily for Shane, Manny didn't like to think too hard about much of anything and decided he was going to ignore the mumbling idiot and move forward with his own part of the plan.

"If you're here already, you might as well go help the shrimp with the money in the back. I'll keep watch over the floor," Manny said, feeling a bit odd giving Cole an order, but he was really acting strange.

"Uh…ok. Yeah, sure." Shane barely responded and made his way to the back of the bank where the smaller guy, who had killed two people without any sign of remorse, had gone, leaving the giant alone in the front.

Moving down the back hall, as he neared the safety-deposit box area, Shane's shock of what he witnessed was making it difficult for him to think or react. He had glimpsed around the corner to see Ray lying there unconscious with the small rat-faced man bending over his body and ripping off what looked like a small key that had been hanging around his motionless friend's neck. Shane hid behind the corner, not entering the room, listening.

"You didn't need to hit him. He was doing as you asked," Shane heard the crippled older man say to the smaller man.

"He wasn't moving fast enough and I hate waiting," Trent replied. Trent looked at his watch, "Right on time. Now, it's time to go open up the piggy bank. That computer nerd had better be ready by now." Shane could hear by the man's voice getting louder that he was heading out of the room back towards the vault. Back towards Shane.

Not wanting to meet eye to eye with this ruthless killer, Shane backed up the hallway as quickly and quietly as he possibly could. He tried to open the nearest door, but it was locked, so he quickly tried another. Mercifully, this one opened. He didn't even bother to look in, before darting through and closing the door behind himself. He held his breath, as he heard Trent pass by seconds later. After waiting for what felt to Shane like an eternity, he started to breathe again and turned to see where he had hidden himself. It was a darkened office, and Shane immediately recognized it, because he had been in this room before. He had eaten many lunches in this room. He was in his friend Ray's office.

Before his eyes could fully adjust to the low light something moved in the darkness, and Shane knew someone else was in the room with him. *Maybe, it's a scared bank employee hiding out like me?* He hoped. "Who's there?" Shane whispered.

The small light on Ray's desk suddenly flicked on, illuminating a man in a suit, calmly sitting in the chair behind Ray's desk.

Mr. Thomas, stared at Shane oddly before asking, "Cole? What are you doing in here? What's going on out there? Is everything going as we had planned?"

– – – – –

Back in the van, Jeff wasn't sure what to do. He looked at the time and knew he was supposed to have killed all the power to the bank over two minutes ago, giving the crew exactly sixty-seconds before the backup power would kick in. Plenty of time for Cole to do what he needed to do.

But everything was all messed up. Cole was nowhere to be found and he was supposed to get the van pulled around to the front of the bank, while the others were getting the money ready in the vault.

Jeff made the decision to do the job he was being paid to do and proceed as planned. He typed on his keyboard and initiated the program to kill the power in the next minute.

Sixty-seconds and everything in that bank would go dark.

– – – – –

Manny heard a loud banging on the front door and walked over to the tinted glass.

It was Cole, now suddenly back and standing outside. Despite his confusion over this, Manny unlocked the door and let him in.

"What the hell? How did you get outside and what's with the change of clothes?" Manny asked, but Cole ignored the moron's questions and ran straight to the back of the bank.

Cole passed by Trent, who was in front of the vault door, key and laptop already in place waiting for the power to be cut.

As Cole entered the hallway, he first ran to the safety-deposit box room and saw Fragile gently tying an unconscious man to one of the tables. Cole turned around without a word, pulled out his gun, and began checking the various doors, slowly making his way down the hallway. Closer towards the door marked with the words, Manager's Office.

As Cole was reaching for the handle, the door opened up and someone came backing out. "I've made a mistake. Sorry. I'll be going now–" Shane spun around, finding himself face-to-face with Cole.

The two young men were virtual mirror images. For a few heartbeats, they both stood there in the brightly lit hallway staring at one another. Cole was wondering how the hell they had found him and Shane thinking he must have completely and utterly lost his mind once and for all.

But before either of them could react or think of what to do next, the lights suddenly went out. They were in total darkness and Shane, out of habit more than anything, pulled out his phone, casting an eerie green light which illuminated long shadows in all directions.

To Shane's horror, the light also illuminated Cole, who raised his gun with one hand and reached out to grab hold of Shane with the other. "Are you lost, replicant, or were you sent here to protect what's inside that envelope?" Cole said as he extended his free hand towards Shane, "Let's find out what you know, shall we?"

Shane gasped, "Wait, don't…" but never got another word out.

The instant Cole's hand made contact with his neck, Shane felt a sudden dizzying flash of light and sound exploding within the room, causing him to drop to his knees. Then, everything went silent and black.

—————

At first, Shane wasn't sure what had happened or how much time had gone by. As he staggered to his feet, his vision was spotted due to the sudden shock to his pupils from the flash and an incessant ringing in his ears that nearly caused him to fall back down to his knees once more. On the ground, he saw something glowing faintly near his foot. It turned out to be his cell phone, dropped when the man with the gun had attacked him. Feeling more than remembering the immediate danger he was in, Shane quickly snatched the phone up and used it to scan the darkness.

Where did that psychopath with the gun go? And, did I imagine it, or did he not look exactly like me? Shane asked himself, but the other man, whoever he was, was nowhere to be found.

Shane took a wobbly step forward, but his foot caught on something. Using the light from his phone, Shane saw a pile of clothing, shoes and a gun. *Did the guy who grabbed me decide to get naked and drop his gun? Yeah, that's normal. What the hell is going on here?* He began to reach down and examine the items more closely when a sudden wave of nausea came over him, nearly causing him to collapse. He stumbled up against the wall, bracing himself.

Shane's head was pounding with what felt like the worst headache of his life. Strangest of all, the thoughts in Shane's mind no longer felt like his own. He felt like another person's life had been crammed inside his brain parallel with his own. His mind was suddenly filled with memories, emotions and feelings, which were completely foreign to him. As if someone were trying to invade his mind and take over.

He stumbled a few steps working to control his unsteady legs beneath him. But, it was not only Shane's mind that was now being altered and affected by what was happening. His brain was also augmenting his body in subtle ways. He felt his strength and posture through a slightly different mind muscle connection become enhanced and corrected. Memories and skills that he now possessed, like considerable martial arts training, were giving him physical cues counter to his usual bookish body mechanics. At any rate, all of it was terribly confusing, and the new memories were giving his body signals Shane was certain he could not perform.

Dizzy with vertigo, Shane felt another wave of nausea come over him again. The core of him felt as if it were being stretched both physically and mentally in two different directions. Knowing real danger was still all around him, he tried as best he could to block it out and concentrate on the more immediate goal of getting out of the bank alive.

Shane's complete panic at this point caused him

to do what most people would do in a similar situation. Run.

Using his cell phone for light, Shane turned a corner and ran directly into the old crippled man whom he had seen earlier with Ray.

"Cole, this is completely out of control. Trent nearly killed that man back there." Fragile nodded his head into the room behind him, referring to the still unconscious Ray, "I mean he hit him with everything he had. We need to reel him in before he elevates this endeavor into something that is totally out of our control." Fragile said as he pulled his own gun out from underneath his tweed coat.

To Shane, the elderly man might as well have been from outer space. The man's proper demeanor did not mesh with the fact the old guy was somehow caught up in all this. *Fragile. His name is Fragile.* The really odd thing was he felt now as if he knew Fragile. Shane had an entire set of new memories about this older man, which were not his own.

Convinced he was caught in a nightmare, Shane fled from Fragile, back the way he had come, and sprinted to escape this horror he found himself in. Shane turned the corner into the hallway, when he heard a nasal laugh sounding a lot like the small rat-looking man who had shot those poor tellers earlier.

Trent. But how do I know the guy's name? Shane never had time to answer his own question.

Shane could not see it, but something, or someone, inside of him recognized the sound of an explosive device bouncing its way down the hallway directly at him.

Run! He reflexively jumped backwards but was stopped by the door leading to the manager's office. His hand grabbed the handle and turned the knob, when the grenade came to a rest no more than a few feet from where he stood. Shane barely had time to duck behind the water fountain when the explosion sent him hurtling backwards towards the wall with so much concussive force it knocked him half-unconscious before he even hit it.

Who is going to take care of the book store? Shane asked himself from somewhere far off in the back of his mind as his body laid crumpled on the floor. The last thing Shane thought he saw before he was enveloped by darkness was an image of himself going back to the bookstore for the rest of the day, where he knew it would be boring, quiet and safe.

— — — — —

Manny carried Shane's unconscious form on one shoulder and two enormous duffle bags filled with cash over the other, like they were nothing more than light grocery bags, across the bank towards the front doors. Trent also had a bag of cash and was dragging another behind him, kicking frightened people out of his way.

Fragile, played the role of the frightened hostage, and having taken the bank key from Manny, made his way to the exit to the blue sedan parked in the handi-cap space directly out front. Not wanting to waste any time, Fragile got into the driver's seat and turned the ignition. Even with Jeff taking the alarms out, the explosion will eventually have the cops here, and Fragile didn't want to be anywhere near this place when that happened.

As novice as he was, Jeff had the foresight to have pulled the van up alongside Fragile's car and waited with the sliding side door open. After depositing the half conscious Shane into the back seat of Fragile's sedan, Manny flung the four bags he and Trent were carrying into the van.

Fragile immediately got out of his car and rummaged through the bags, searching for the envelope Cole and he had been after. But, other than a whole lot of cash, Fragile found nothing inside the four bags.

The envelope must be in one of the remaining two bags still inside the bank. Looking down at the pale and unconscious man whom he took to be Cole, Fragile decided under the current circumstances, finding the envelope could wait until they were back at the safe house. Trent's loud deviation from the plan was going to bring the heat upon them very quickly.

Fragile noticed that Jeff himself looked very pale and worried behind the driver's seat of the van. Jeff stared at Shane in the back seat of Fragile's car and did not take his eyes off of him. Because Fragile had dismissed the possibility, Jeff alone knew there had actually been two people inside the bank who looked identical to one another. He had been watching the whole event go down on the video surveillance cameras.

While Manny and Trent went back into the bank for the remaining two bags of cash. Fragile rolled his window down and spoke to the scared young computer prodigy.

"Jeff, you alright, son? You don't look so good." Fragile glanced back at Shane in the back seat. "I'm going to take Cole back to the safe house, and I'll meet you there. No reason to think that part of the plan has gone to hell. Tell those other two the plan stays the same, until we can get a hold of Wayne and have enough time to figure out what the hell happened in there." Fragile did not wait for Jeff's reply before putting the car in gear and driving away. If he had he would have heard the almost shell-shocked Jeff say, "But that's not Cole!"

A short time later, Manny and Trent came out, Manny carrying two more bags and Trent following behind with a vicious snarl on his face.

"Get out of that seat. I'm driving," Trent growled at Jeff, who immediately jumped out of the driver's seat and into the back with his computer equipment and gear.

Manny flung the two remaining bags, making six in total, into the back, before sliding the door closed and getting into the passenger seat next to Trent.

Frightened as he was of these two, Jeff spoke, "Fragile said to meet back at the safe house as planned, and that there is no reason to think that it's been com-promised. He said we should wait for Wayne to see what to do next." As Trent drove the van out of the strip mall heading towards the freeway entrance.

"Fragile? That cripple ain't my boss. And neither is that Mr. Tough Guy Cole. Thinks he's Bruce Lee or something. Well big deal I say. Manny here is a black-belt in Tang Soo Do too and he could crush Cole like a twig. He'll be lucky I don't slit his throat the next time I see him." Trent did indeed look to Jeff like he needed to desperately open up someone's throat.

Jeff watched as Trent turned onto the freeway entrance going the opposite direction of the safe house.

"Hey, Trent, isn't it the other way to the safe house? I think you're going the wrong way," However, as Jeff spoke the words he quickly realized what was happening.

Trent and Manny are stealing the money from the others. Jeff's fears now grew for reasons other than getting caught by the police. In many ways, Jeff was young and naive, but even he could tell that whatever happened next was not going to be good.

"Oh yeah, didn't you know kid? Manny and I have got our own safe house. Don't we, big guy?" Trent giggled a maniac's laugh, as he grinned at Manny. Confirming Jeff's suspicions.

For his part, Manny simply sat there quietly in his seat. His eyes and face were set in deep thought, an unnatural look for the big brute. Trent snapped his fingers in front of his friend's face, trying to get him to lighten up.

"Hey Manny, what's wrong with you, bro? We knew this was going to get ugly one way or another. By changing the plan, Cole simply got the ball rolling for us a little earlier than expected. That's all." Trent gave one more theatrical snap of his fingers followed by a flip of the bird, before removing his hand from in front of Manny's face.

Still, Manny neither responded nor reacted. He sat there white as a ghost.

"You know… now that I'm thinking about it," Trent went on, choosing to ignore his big friend, "things might have worked out even better than we had planned. We got the cash and we got the computer geek with his fancy gear. I bet the nerd could help us with our 'travel arrangements' even better than we could. Ain't that right, Jeffrey?" Trent smiled. He was liking this new plan that was forming. Trent looked into the rearview mirror and to his sadistic delight, Jeff's petrified eyeballs stared back at him. The computer hacker's terror painted an even broader grin on the psychopath's face.

Jeff thought he had never seen a face quite like Trent's before. Trent's was a face bent on destruction and self-loathing. This small man hated himself every bit as much as he hated the world.

Trent's voice dripped with sarcasm, when he said, "Hey geek, did I tell you when we met how happy I am you're part of the team."

CHAPTER 8
COLE'S STORY

Years ago…

It was less than three weeks after the final adoption papers had come through that a young Cole had found himself on a plane headed to an air force base located on the island of Guam.

Cole's new father was a Pararescueman, also known as a 'PJ'. Pararescuemen are United States Air Force Special Operations Command (AFSOC) and Air Combat Command (ACC) operatives who are tasked with the recovery and medical treatment of personnel in extremely hostile combat environments. Pararescue personnel are highly trained specialists who perform extremely hazardous duties demanding of the very highest mental and physical discipline. Among this elite group, Cole's father was among the best there was. Their motto, "That Other's May Live" is a creed they lived and breathed and their bravery is virtually legendary among all of the branches of the military. If you were a GI out in the field of combat and somehow found yourself needing to be rescued, it was someone like Staff Sergeant Henry 'Hank' Wiseman who came and got you.

As a result, Cole would spend the next eight years moving around the world to the various military bases his father would be stationed out of as was typical, especially a member of an elite Special Operations unit like Henry was a part, of a military family.

It was upon arriving at that first air base, Cole immediately saw that there were kids already out on the street. Mostly boys with a few scattered sisters mixed in between. They were black, white, Hispanic and Asian. A mixed pot and maybe a little over a dozen of them. All from military families. These were going to be his new neighbors and the naïve Cole was excited to go out and play with them.

He quickly dropped his things in his new bedroom, pulled on some swim shorts, his plastic flip-flop sandals and was out the door headed towards the community pool that was located at the upper east corner of the base's housing area.

However, he never made it to the swimming pool that day. Up ahead of Cole, along the long stretch of identical houses, the other kids saw him coming with his bright orange flip-flops and big smile. They slowly began moving away from their yards and front porches, into the center of the street to greet him. The kids formed a loose line, which quickly became a circle around him, blocking Cole's path to the pool. Some of them, the bigger ones, were as old as fifteen or sixteen while the others were younger, around Cole's age. The younger ones stood behind their older brothers and sisters. Waiting.

They were excited to welcome Cole to the neighborhood and they were going to do it with their knuckles and feet. First, it was the larger older boys who rained down punches and kicks upon him soon followed by the smaller ones and even some of the girls. Luckily for Cole, they quickly grew bored or maybe tired of punishing the boy curled up in a fetal position and returned to their respective homes along the street.

When he stumbled home barefoot, one of the other kids must have taken his orange sandals as a trophy, his mother screamed out in horror as she wrapped her arms around her baby boy, "Oh Cole! What happened? Who did this to you? I'm going to go out there right now and have a word with their mothers. And if I happen to get my hands on one of those filthy little monsters myself, I'm going to–"

"Linda, calm down and just hold him. You'll do nothing of the sort." Henry said to his almost hysterical wife. "You'll only make things tougher for Cole, the next time he goes out there and has to face them." His father explained to his wife, "Now come here boy and let's have a look at the damage they did to you. Linda, could you please get me my Dit Da Jow medicine? It might still be packed in my bags."

As his wife went to their bedroom to fetch the ancient Chinese medicine, Henry went to the kitchen sink and returned with a warm soapy rag to clean Cole's wounds. He let out a soft whistle as he assessed the numerous cuts and bruises the other kids had given his son. "Let's start with how many there were… I'm guessing more than ten and less than fifteen? And around your age but some were much older, trying to show the younger ones how tough they are. Am I correct?" Henry asked.

"Yeah, I think so… something like that." Cole

said. His bloodied lips were already swelling and it hurt to say too much.

"I guess this means we'll have to begin your training in the Fu even sooner than I thought." Sergeant Wiseman told his son with a slight chuckle. By 'the Fu', Cole's father was referring to Kung Fu.

Besides being highly trained as a P.J., Henry was a fourth generation disciple of Grandmaster Lee Shiem Cheung of Jook Lum Gee Tong Long Pai (Bamboo Temple Southern Praying Mantis Kung Fu), the most difficult to master and deadliest of all martial art systems. This unique martial art is a close range, energy-borrowing system, designed to defeat larger and multiple attackers at once.

Henry had come across this once secretive Hakka art over fifteen years prior, when he was stationed out of Lackland Air Force Base in Texas. Since then he had become a Sifu or 'teacher' himself and even trained his fellow pararescue jumpers in a simplified version of the kung fu system, which he affectionately dubbed the Dragon Combat System, hoping if they should ever need it, perhaps it might help save their lives.

It was apparent to Henry that his son was going to need to arm himself mentally and physically if he was going to survive the bullies that inevitably would occupy the streets of a military base. Henry knew for Cole, this was the first test of many more to come. But it would also be the last in which his son was the only one to walk away bloodied and bruised. Cole trained Southern Praying Mantis Kung Fu every day. From that day forward no matter how many there happened to be, it was Cole who was the one left standing and not requiring medical treatment of some kind.

Growing up and constantly being shuffled around to different bases, Cole was always the new kid. He never felt as if he fit in with the other kids his age. School was more like a prison or a combat zone for Cole. It was not a place for him to learn, it was a place to do battle. It was non-stop fighting for him causing him to become a loner. No matter how much love and support his parents would give him, Cole felt very lonely and very different. He knew he was strange to the other kids and an outcast. Other than training Kung Fu, Cole had no hope, no desires, and no passion. By the time he was seventeen he started to believe that nothing made a difference and it didn't matter if he lived or died. Nobody would miss him anyway.   That was around the time he met Shelby.

— — — — —

"Watcha doing?" She asked, peeking over the side of the fence.

"Practicing my Kung Fu." Cole thought it kind of obvious considering he was hitting a wooden Wing Chun dummy at that particular moment, "What are you doing, besides spying on people in their own backyards?" Cole asked.

"That's like a type of Karate or something, right?" Shelby deflected with another question, completely ignoring Cole's rude reply.

"Yeah, something like that." He said, "Except there are no belts. Karate is a martial art–a system of fighting. Kung Fu is different. It translates to 'hard work' and refers to anything that you have to practice. It can be anything that requires a lot of patience, energy, and time to complete. My dad always says my mom has good Kung Fu after he eats her cooking."

"Cool." Shelby said, gracefully jumping into his yard and clearly disregarding the fact that Cole was trying to concentrate and practice. "Well–not really, it kinda sounds boring actually." She added.

"Then why are you standing there watching me do it?" Cole kept moving through his practice as he spoke, but was clearly distracted.

"I guess I'm just trying to figure out which one is the dummy." Shelby teased, "Besides, I'm new to the base and you're my next door neighbor." She replied, "I'm Shelby by the way."

"Don't you have something better to do, Shelby?" Cole asked.

"Absolutely, but I figured you needed some company. You'll soon find that I'm a really giving person. And your name is?"

"You're sincerity is admirable." Cole was beginning to like this girl's quick wit, but he was still weary that this was a set up of some kind. But realizing he hadn't given her his name he quickly added, "Cole. My name is Cole Wiseman."

"Nice to meet you Cole." she said, "But I've already seen you around. This is only my first week here, and I think I've seen you get into three fights at school already. Call me crazy, but I think it's important to know if I'm living next to some kind of psychopath or something. Wouldn't you agree?"

"I'm not a psychopath. I'm a high functioning sociopath," Cole said defensively. "Two of those fights I was only trying to get to my locker. That other one… Well, they were picking on that little freshman kid, and it pissed me off."

"Oh so you're a hero or something, is that it? Fighting for the underdog? Saving the day and coming to the rescue for those too weak to fight for themselves." She was very direct. "So I guess those kids you beat up had it coming." She said, her words dripping with sarcasm. "Don't you like to have any real fun?" She asked.

"Kung Fu is fun. Breaking bullies in half is fun." He replied honestly. "You have to admit it was pretty metal the way I worked those guys." Cole laughed thinking he had a comrade in Shelby.

However, the look she gave him was not one of approval.

"Oh come on!" Cole pleaded not wanting to seem the bully. "You know I was outnumbered and they attacked me first."

"Ok, clearly you're not picking up what I am putting down, so let me try this line of questioning a different way. Do you like to have any fun that doesn't involve maiming or hurting others?"

Cole stood there silent.

"Have you ever stopped to consider the fact that you might be the bully?"

"What the hell are you talking about? If they were older and there were more of them, how am I the bully in that situation?" He couldn't believe the audacity of this girl.

"Well… I guess the obvious question would be, do you think ANY of those other boys have ever studied Kung Fu? Are any of them trained to kick some serious ass like you are? Have you ever even asked yourself that before?" She knew she had him then by the look on his face. So she pressed on, "No? I think not. But you ARE trained and you use it against everyone who might object to your sense of right and wrong. Have you ever stopped to consider the fact that these 'bullies' might simply be playing out a normal sociological coming of age pattern. Trying to find their place in the pack if you will. And along comes Cole, the mighty champion of the underdog and oppressed. Removing teeth and breaking bones along the way, I might add."

"What are you some kind of word magician?" Cole was certain he had never met anyone like this girl in his life.

"No. But close, I'm a Ninja." She answered. "And I'm applying empathy to the situation. You should try it some time."

Again, Cole was at a complete loss of words. Intrigued by her different view of the situation, this new girl was unusual and this impressed Cole.

"How's the beach here? Pretty cool we're only a short walk away." She asked, changing the subject suddenly. Cole would learn she tended to do that often. Her mind was quick.

"I wouldn't know. Haven't been there." Cole replied.

"What? Are you kidding me? How long have you lived here?"

"Around six months." Cole answered.

"You mean to tell me you've lived here almost half a year and you haven't gone to the beach even once?" She asked incredulous at even the possibility.

"Yup, I'm avoiding confrontation. I tend to attract trouble with the locals." Cole answered honestly. At this point this was more peer interaction than he had in over four years.

"Well, were going today." She stood up heading back to the fence, "Go get some swim trunks and a beach towel. I want company, and considering I don't know anyone here, you'll have to do." She teased, as she jumped back over the fence to her own yard.

"Hey," Cole called over the fence, "You're pretty good at that," Noting how easily she had hurtled herself over an eight foot fence.

She poked her head over the top one last time, "Parkour baby!"

"What's that?" Cole asked.

"It's a sport. Like running and gymnastics all in one." She replied, "I guess you could say it's a type of Kung Fu, and if you play your cards right, I might even teach you how to do it." She gave him a wink when she said this, turning to go inside to change into a bathing suit.

"Hey Shelby, one more question…" He asked, now it was his turn to pop his head over the fence.

"Why me?"

"Who knows? Maybe I like charity cases." She said over her shoulder heading into her house to go get a beach towel. "Not to mention, I think you're kinda cute. Meet you outside in five." She giggled before disappearing inside her house.

I think you're kinda cute too. Cole smiled to himself, dropping back down off the fence and running inside to get his own towel.

They were as opposite as two people could get. Where Cole was overly serious and intense, Shelby was always joking and making light of situations. Yin and Yang.

Cole was seventeen years old and at last had his first friend. The two were virtually inseparable from that day on.

— — — — —

At age eighteen, Cole followed in his father's footsteps and enlisted in the military, albeit a different branch and specialty. Where his father had been trained to rescue and save lives, Cole's particular area of expertise was in the taking of them.

Cole was in his third year of active duty when tragedy struck in the form of an automobile accident, robbing Cole of both his parents simultaneously.

The one consolation to the tragedy was that at least his parents had the opportunity to meet and grow to love Shelby, who would become his wife less than a year later. Cole often would claim he wouldn't know what he would have done had he not had Shelby during that awful time.

For the next couple of years the two lived happily together on various military bases around the world much in parallel to his own parents. When not on mission the two would spend all the time they could with each other and at night in bed, as couples often tended to do, would plan the rest of their lives together. Trying to imagine what life would be like after Cole got out of active service.

— — — — —

Not long after getting out of his own tours in the military, Cole was finding the job market not quite as warm and inviting to veterans as the military had led on. Despite his considerable military expertise, Cole, along with his wife Shelby found themselves struggling to pay the bills each month. They had mistakenly trusted a financial advisor with some bad investments that turned out to be not quite the 'sure things' that had been promised and had left them nearly broke.

Cole was forced to get the first job that came along, working as a security guard for a jewelry store in Chicago's Washington Park district. Shelby, having grown used to the safe and secure life of a military base, did not like living a couple of blocks away on the fourth floor of a one-bedroom apartment in the middle of one of the worst parts of the city. Cole had tried to ease his wife's fear of the neighborhood by the fact of how close he would be and that the situation was only temporary.

"Just until I get a better job," he told her.

Unfortunately, the better job didn't come in time to prevent Shelby from becoming another statistic in the city's murder, rape and robbery rate.

When Cole was called home in the early morning hours and as horrible as the scene was, he noticed immediately by their callous demeanor that the police were going to spend as little energy on the case as possible. The cops had knocked on a few doors in the apartment complex and asked if anyone had heard or seen anything, but they had quickly given up before even reaching the end of the hallway. They spent more time checking on Cole's alibi of working at the jewelry store that night than actually investigating who might have actually committed the heinous murder of his beloved wife. Atrocities that only monsters could have committed, all for what seemed like a few meager items and possessions.

"You understand," the investigating cop had told Cole, "it often times turns out to be the husband or boyfriend who commits these kind of crimes. We're just being thorough and checking everything, which reminds me, is there any chance that your wife might have had a boyfriend or something on the side, while you were working all those late nights?"

Cole nearly punched the cop in the throat at the comment. Instead, Cole did what he had learned during his time in the military: He agreed to accompany the officers down to the station and fill out a report and waited patiently. He listened to the officers carefully taking in the facts and began devising a plan with only one thing on his mind. Revenge.

Cole was no detective but, for some reason, he felt certain of one thing. The person who murdered his wife lived in the apartment complex.

He believed this for a couple of reasons: One, whoever had done this knew when Cole would be at work. They must have watched his comings and goings enough to know his schedule and routine. Two, because Shelby, out of fear of the neighborhood, had rarely stepped foot outside of the apartment, whoever had done this knew that she was even there. After all, Shelby and Cole hadn't been there very long, and the murderer must have watched them moving in. So, the question was: how to flush the rat out of its nest?

Cole's plan was simple. He knew predators liked familiar hunting grounds and easy victims, so he decided to make himself the most appetizing bait he could.

He did not wish to go back to the apartment, but he knew he had to in order for his plan to work. So after returning from the police station, Cole entered the apartment resolving himself to what had now become a house of horrors to him.

Like his father had taught him so many years ago, Cole wanted to confront his fears head on and went directly to the bedroom. He stood in silence directly where his wife had died just hours prior. He quietly took in details like the wooden floorboards underneath him that were still slightly damp and giving off an acidic odor from the solvent cleaner the forensics unit had used in an attempt to clean up some of the blood.

The signs of a brutal assault and murder and the subsequent police investigation were everywhere. It was clear from the carnage that Shelby had put up a fight. *Good girl.* Cole thought to himself.

Despite his tremendous self-control, being there proved to be too much for him and in his sudden rage he picked up the bed mattress and threw it clear across the room. He then proceeded to destroy everything else that wasn't already ruined in the room, before collapsing on the floor. But before total despair could grab root of him, he noticed something on the floor and picked it up. A knife.

He had always kept it hidden underneath his mattress and he was thankful it was not stolen along with everything else. It was his father's PJLT, or Pararescue Jumper's light Combat, Search, and Rescue Tactical Knife. Cole held the knife in his hand carefully admiring it's non-reflecting 440C high chromium stainless steel blade with vampire rip-teeth serrations and top length spine swages. The fixed blade was designed with the right geometry and balance to be extremely useful to the rescue service skill, while retaining the characteristics to be a seriously formidable weapon when needed. The blade was built to both save and kill. The PJLT had proven itself in the field of combat, service, and rescue across the wide range of tactical and rescue service and his father along with the extensive Kung Fu and military training had taught Cole how to handle the weapon well. It was the knife he had used through more than six years of combat and at this point felt like an extension to his hand. Holding the blade again in his hands infused him with the ice that normally coursed through his veins. He had his mission and he felt sorry for anyone who tried to get in his way.

He waited a couple of weeks then took out a couple of credit cards and purchased a lot of expensive electronics, including a computer, a flat screen TV, a sound system, musical instruments, sports memorabilia and equipment. Anything the cards could buy before maxing out. Anything and everything that could easily be picked up and sold on the black market or at nearby pawnshops without too many questions being asked. Cole was sure to make himself extremely noticeable when he was moving all of the stuff into the apartment and told the neighbors across the hall that he was buying it as a method of grieving. He also purchased some micro GPS tracking unit systems from an old military buddy of his, who sold that kind of equipment online. Cole installed the trackers in all of the lavish equipment.

Night after night, he went to work and waited. It didn't take long. It didn't even take a full week, before Cole's entire place was ransacked and completely cleaned out.

Now, it was time for the second phase of his plan. That next day, Cole called into work sick then proceeded to work on the wireless tablet he had purchased along with the GPS equipment. He double clicked the software application that would activate the GPS transmitters. Sure enough, the transmitters were giving off their little bleeps, revealing the thief's location not more than a hundred yards from where Cole sat

in his apartment. The person or persons were definitely in the same building. Cole made a quick mental
note of the approximate location of where the apartment would be, pocketed the small wireless tablet and
walked out of his front door heading for the stairwell.

Exiting the elevator on the third floor, Cole
counted his paces as he walked down the hallway and
approached the door to what he guessed to be the
correct apartment. He would need to know the approximate distance once he was back outside on the
fire-escape. As he passed the door, Cole could hear
the sound of loud rap music, probably coming from
the same sound system that had been in his apartment
days earlier. His adrenaline was pumping now and he
used his old Kung Fu and chi kung training to filter
into his mind in order to control his breathing and slow
his suddenly accelerating heart rate.

Gotcha. Cole smiled briefly, as he proceeded on to
the elevator doors and went up one floor, back to his
own apartment.

He had confirmed the location of this new thief,
but Cole still had to be sure it was the same person
who had robbed and murdered his wife. This would
mean finding the person and some sort of evidence
from the original crime.

He put on the all black fatigues he had purchased
from the military supply store and pocketed his father's
knife. Once armed and ready he then climbed out onto
the fire escape of his apartment and made his way
down to where he assumed he would be close enough
to the thief's apartment to have a look inside the win-

dows.

Cole was grateful that someone climbing around the fire escape at night wouldn't arouse too much suspicion. The kids in the apartment complex used them all of the time to sneak out or smoke their cigarettes or joints. He was actually kind of surprised to find that he was completely alone out there this particular night.

He made it to the outside of the apartment quietly and without incident. The music inside was so loud that it probably would have hidden any sounds Cole might have made anyway.

Next, Cole pulled out a small mirror that had a telescoping handle on it for his first look inside the apartment. What he saw made his blood boil. Then, it turned cold as ice.

The first thing Cole saw, on the dresser in front of the window, was his Army Service Uniform with the 'Ranger' tab clearly showing on the upper left sleeve. The uniform had been stolen the night of his wife's murder and had been the only material loss that had even crossed Cole's mind. Now, he had all of the confirmation he needed to be certain he had the murderer's apartment.

Cole next saw not one but two men in the apartment. One, an obese slob of a man, was fast asleep, despite the blaring music in the living room, an empty bottle of Jack Daniel's whiskey at the foot of his bed. Cole shifted the mirror slightly and saw the other man, smoking out of an enormous bong, sitting on the couch and watching a basketball game on the flat screen TV that had been in Cole's living room just a day earlier.

Cole continued over to the bathroom window to scan the rest of the apartment for signs of anyone else.

Nobody, only these two pieces of trash. Cole's plan to do some surveillance and then return to his apartment to conduct phase three of his plan quickly dissolved, as he saw the last item he remembered buying for his wife on the shelf next to the filthy bathroom sink. It was a dragonfly necklace that he had purchased from his boss, using up an entire paycheck, even with the small discount the small Persian man had given him.

"Oh, Cole! It's one of the most gorgeous things I've ever laid eyes on. But we can't afford this. It must have cost you a fortune. Maybe you should return it." Shelby chastised her husband.

"Shelby, you are the most gorgeous thing I've ever laid eyes on. That's just a piece of sparkly metal, but when I saw it at the shop I knew I had to get it for you. It's a one of a kind like you and I specifically saved for it. Life is too short not to say and do exactly what you feel. Besides, I have never spent our money recklessly on things we can't afford and look where that has gotten us." Cole joked. Cole could still remember reassuring Shelby that they could afford it and even if they couldn't she was worth every penny and more as he placed it on his wife's neck where it remained until the day she died.

Shelby had loved dragonflies and would tell him factoids with regards to the little critters. "Did you know that they have been around for over two hundred and forty-million years and some live their entire life in only twenty-four hours?" She would exclaim.

The sight of the necklace was too much for Cole. He quickly moved back to the bedroom window, which was slightly cracked and slid it slowly and quietly open with his gloved fingers. He crouched down low so as not to be seen from the other room. He could hear the fat man's loud snores over the blaring music. Cole's mind was racing now. He had not planned to act immediately but was now in the room and fully committed to what he was going to do next.

He slid his father's knife from his pocket and shoved it smoothly into the sleeping man's throat. Cole chose to stick the man precisely in the place he knew would take the longest time to choke the man to death on his own blood. Cole, while in the military, had seen the process take several minutes. He hoped it took as long as possible. The blood gargling was barely audible over the cacophony blasting from the television, as Cole pulled the knife from the man's throat and, in one fluid movement, crossed from the bed to the door. In an instant, Cole was on top of the other man, slamming the man's head straight into the glass table in front of him.

"Hi there, can you guess what time it is?" Cole asked with a snarl. "Payback time, Asshole! Now, why don't you take a little nap, while I get everything ready for us to have a good time?" He had the man's head still in his hands. Without waiting for a reply, Cole smashed his fist down onto the man's face, using the bottom of his hand like a hammer, knocking the guy out cold. He was a ferocious beast, some kind of animal of pure darkness and horror. This was the reckoning. This was Cole's revenge.

Cole had killed for the United States Army, but never for himself. He was one of the good guys. A hero. But now Cole was a villain; and he relished every bit of it. He took his time with the process and, before he was done, learned every excruciating detail about Shelby's death. He didn't want to hear it but found he needed to know what she had gone through in her last moments of life. Their pain was a sort of catharsis to his own loss.

He also learned that the two men were brothers, Burt and Steve Wilson. The fat one, suffocating on his own blood in the bedroom, was Burt. Steve, still thinking he was going to somehow survive this, told Cole anything he asked. Cole learned the Wilson brothers were small time drug dealers who pushed cocaine, heroin and meth for a guy named Rodney Lewis. They were robbing apartments to pay for their own habit, so Rodney wouldn't find out they were using up all of his product, before it could hit the streets.

So drugs killed Shelby. *My wife died for nothing. Smoke for addicts who are too lazy to do anything else with their lives.* Cole thought to himself.

He cleaned the place of anything that would link these two corpses to him. It took a little over an hour to take all of his own items back up to his apartment. He was extra cautious not to be seen in the process. One good thing about living in such a dangerous part of the city was that people, once they were holed up in their apartments, pretty much stayed put and kept their nose out of their neighbor's business. This rule was especially true after the sun went down.

When he was done, Cole locked the front door, left the Wilson's apartment and climbed through the same window he had entered. But not before he had recovered his old Rangers uniform and his wife's dragonfly necklace. Stealing a last glance through the window, as he ascended the fire escape, he could see Burt's eyes fixed in death, staring directly at him. Cole gave him a wink and scaled the stairs quickly back up to his own apartment.

Cole took the drugs, cash and two guns he had found from the Wilson's place as well as their boss's phone number and address. He wasn't quite sure why, but at one point during the interrogation, Cole had decided to pay Mr. Lewis a visit too.

Without deliberating on the decision, Cole checked and loaded one of the guns, one with a highly illegal silencer threaded on it, along with the extra loaded magazine he had found for it. He concealed it within his black fatigues and got into his car.

Driving the thirty minutes to the address Steve had given him for Rodney Lewis, Cole had already begun to shape yet another plan. He parked across from the only house with lights on inside at this hour of the night and dialed Lewis' cell number.

"Who the hell is calling me from a blocked number?" answered a voice from the other end.

"Mr. Lewis, my name is Cole. Two of your associates, Burt and Steve, stole from me and, as a result, are both now dead. But, it turns out they were also stealing from you. Your product…" Cole let the words trail off, allowing them to sink in. "Though I don't know how much there was originally, I figured you would want what's left. I have it and really have no use for it. I'm willing to sell it back to you. At a great price, of course. Twenty-five thousand dollars. Let's call it a finder's fee." Cole had to keep from chuckling. He was actually enjoying himself. Knowing from the now deceased Steve exactly how much the stuff was worth, approximately four times that, Cole had chosen an amount that would fool Lewis into thinking that Cole had no idea what he was doing. Just some jerk-off who had rolled a couple of mid-level dealers and was hoping to score big time.

"What a good little boy scout you must be," Lewis replied. "You think you're gonna sell my own shit back to me? You must be stupid or crazy, if you think I'm gonna–"

"Your alternative is that I simply hang up now and flush the shit down the toilet," Cole interrupted. "The choice is completely up to you. As I said before, I have no use for it."

The silence on the other end told Cole his plan was going to work.

"When and where do you want to do this?" Lewis eventually answered.

"How about right now? I don't want to hold this crap any longer than I have to." Cole hoped to sound a little nervous now. He gave Lewis the address to a late night diner to meet at barely five minutes away. Cole told him they could do the deal in the parking lot. Exactly the kind of place an amateur, not knowing what the hell he was doing, would choose.

"I'll send a guy over there right now," Lewis said.

"Good, I'll be waiting, wearing a blue football jersey. Number 12. If you're not there in thirty minutes, I'm gone - and your stuff along with me." Cole hung up without waiting for a reply.

Within fifteen minutes, two large men emerged followed by a smaller man who locked up the house behind them. The big man on the left was carrying a small duffle bag. He got into a car and backed out of the driveway. The other big guy got behind the wheel of the white SUV and waited for the smaller man, Lewis, to climb into the passenger side.

Three of them. This is going to be easier than I expected. Cole thought to himself.

He waited patiently for the car and the SUV to drive along the block and turn the corner. As soon as they were out of sight, Cole slipped out of his car and ran to Lewis' house. He easily scaled the back fence, taking note of the BEWARE of DOG sign. He dropped into the backyard and had his knife out before his feet had even hit the ground. His military training kicked into overdrive. He dispatched the charging dog without even breaking stride to the backdoor of the house. He had to move quickly, if his plan was going to go smoothly.

Unsure if the house was completely empty, Cole stealthily came in through a window, after checking the room with his telescoping mirror. He went silently room-to-room, like he had hundreds of times in the military. Empty.

Now, he proceeded to set up his little surprise for Lewis, for when the drug dealer returned.

As Cole had expected, Lewis returned loud and angry, having been stood up on the meeting to get back his drugs. He was practically screaming, as he unlocked the front door, dropped his keys at the small table next to the coat closet, where Cole had concealed himself, and kept walking into the room.

The other two men could be heard entering into the room. The sound of the front door shutting and being locked could barely be heard over their boss's ranting. Cole tightened then loosened and relaxed his grip on the pistol, as he watched the shadow of one guard move past the closet then the other guard's shadow move past.

Here we go. Cole thought as he pushed the closet door open with his shoulder and gripped the gun with both hands. Against Cole, the three men didn't stand a chance.

The two big men spun around in surprise. Clearly caught off guard by the speed of the attack and the natural tendency of people to feel comfort in their own home environment.

A single bullet went into the left eye of the big man, who was still holding the duffle bag Cole had seen earlier. Without hesitation, Cole shot a double-tap into the other guard's chest and one into his head, turning the man off like a light switch.

Rodney Lewis turned in shock and confusion, attempting to escape. When Cole grabbed his arm, he tried to scream, but Cole pistol-whipped Rodney, snapping his jawbone. Rodney's entire upper body, including his head, made a loud crunch noise as he fell to the ground killing him on impact.

Cole didn't have a real motivation or purpose for what he was doing at this point. His life was ripped from him and simply gone. He wanted to keep hurting bad people like this. He took even bigger loot from Rodney's house with no clear plan of what to do next.

Three hours later, Cole, a changed man, was back in his apartment. He had ruthlessly tortured and killed five men in a less than six hours, and Cole felt nothing. No satisfaction, as he had first thought he would. No remorse for the brutality. Neither guilt nor pleasure. Cole felt nothing at all.

He undressed and showered; barely feeling the water hit his body. He got into the bed he used to share with his now dead wife. The sheets felt cold and alien to him, without her giggly form there to make it home.

Despite his complete exhaustion, Cole could not sleep. After a time, he watched the first light from a new day coming through the cracks of the closed blinds in the window.

That was when he began to cry. Uncontrolled tears streaked down his face pooling in the hollow part of his neck, as he lay on his back unable to move or wipe them away.

That morning, Cole wept for his dead wife. He wept for the life they had planned together. The life that would never be. Since this entire nightmare had all begun, for the first and last time, Cole wept for himself.

- - - - -

In the following days, Cole quit his job, putting in his two-week notice so as to not arouse any questions that simply disappearing would have caused. He paid his rent for the rest of the month, but was out by the end of the week.

It was the last home Cole would ever live in. From that day forward, he would check in and out of rented hotels, never staying in one place for longer than it took him to shower and sleep. Cole returned to his apartment for the last time, taking only three personal items: his old uniform, the dragonfly necklace that he had recovered from the newly deceased Wilson brothers and his father's knife.

Getting rid of the drugs for some cash turned out to be easier than Cole had initially suspected. Despite having no previous experience with buying or selling drugs, but by putting the word out that he had some "good shit at a great price," a business formed quickly around him. In this way, he kept finding new dealers and dispatched them, as he had with Rodney Lewis. Cole found pushers and users easy enough to manipulate, and he routinely ripped them off, killing everyone involved. In the ensuing weeks and months, Cole had done more to disrupt the local drug trade than law enforcement could have hoped to achieve in years.

Cole later believed this is what led him to hooking up with Wayne. Wayne's business was information and never got involved with drugs directly. However, he worked around the edges of so many peripheral criminal activities that it was not long before he heard rumors that someone was offing drug dealers. Cole assumed the reports that there was a vigilante or group out there killing drug dealers for no apparent reason had intrigued Wayne and caused him to seek Cole out.

Indeed, for Wayne, finding Cole, as it turned out, was the easy part. Keeping track of him, as it always was, proved to be more difficult than initially anticipated. The guy kept moving from hotel to hotel. Wayne had put three separate tails on him to keep from losing the former soldier.

More importantly, how to approach Cole without him fleeing or killing you was going to prove tricky.

Wayne used information and manipulation to get what he wanted. He needed to know more about this man before he could make a move on him. He needed to know what Cole's real motivation was. Once he knew that, he could twist and bend Cole to his will.

Wayne left a sealed envelope at the front desk of Cole's current hotel with a simple message along with a contact phone number:

For every drug pusher you take out, two will take over in their place. If you really want to do something interesting and effective, give me a call. -Wayne

After the envelope was delivered, Cole disappeared from his room. Wayne's guys had no idea where he had gone. He simply vanished.

Two days later, Wayne got the call.

"Who are you and what do you want from me?" Cole's voice asked calmly over the line.

"I am merely a guy who appreciates all of the work you are doing, cleaning up the neighborhood, shall we say," Wayne coyly responded, waiting a beat before he continued, "but you have been taking down bigger and bigger operations. I think it's only a matter of time before someone gets in a lucky shot and takes you down. Plus, if I can find you, what makes you think others can't do the same?"

"Go on," was all Cole replied.

"I'm offering you an opportunity to do what you are doing but with perhaps a little more structure and direction," Wayne said.

"How do I know you're not law enforcement or one of the dirt bags I'm hunting who's looking for an opportunity to kill me?" asked Cole.

"Because if I was and I knew where you were, don't you think you would be in jail or dead already? I'd have sent you a little more than just a message to contact me, don't you think?"

Cole's silence was an affirmative to Wayne, so he pressed on, "Come on, your smart enough to see what's coming next. You're heading towards a brick wall at a hundred miles an hour. Someone's eventually gonna put a bullet in your head. I'm suggesting we meet and have a little chat. You can choose the place. Sit down. Have a coffee. You might be surprised to find how much we could benefit each other. My name is Wayne Daniels. Ask around and find out more about me, if you like. Then, call me back, if you're interested." Wayne let that one sink in a little.

He was going to say something else, but before he could speak, Cole said, "Sure. Ok, I'll be in touch, Wayne," and hung up the line.

Damn. Wayne thought to himself.

He would have liked to have learned a little bit more to manipulate the kid with. As it turned out, however, he didn't have to. Cole called him back a couple of days later with a time and place to meet.

Wayne arrived ten minutes early at the crowded coffee shop Cole had chosen. He purchased a caramel latte and found a seat at the only table available. As Wayne sat down, a blonde man seated himself at the table across from him.

"You're early." Cole said to him with a smile that was not at all friendly.

"So are you, it appears." Wayne was going to mirror him a while. He didn't want to do or say anything that would cause Cole to bolt. Taking it slowly could yield information that Wayne could use later in the conversation.

Wayne sensed right away that this young man would kill without hesitation or question. That much he saw when he looked into Cole's lifeless eyes. Whatever had happened to him had left him soulless. Wayne could see Cole had a death wish and was upping the stakes higher and higher, until he found someone who would or could put him out of his misery. In addition, he was obviously well trained ex-military by the way he acted. Most important, he was highly enthusiastic to get his hands bloody. In contrast, Wayne never got his hands dirty, always using others to get his jobs done for him. Cole was perfect for Wayne.

"Hello, Wayne Daniels. I heard you are a guy who works with information. Never actually doing anything for yourself, keeping your hands nice and clean. You prefer to simply put the pieces of information together with the right operators and take a part of the resulting action." Cole had found out a lot in a very short time. "So, am I correct in assuming you want to add me as another pawn to the little chess game that you like to play?" Cole asked, becoming quickly uninterested.

How the hell did he find out all of that? Wayne thought to himself.

"Not a pawn, young man. No, with your obvious talents, I see you more as a knight," Wayne complemented, using Cole's chess metaphor and quickly adding, "but you'll have to pay your dues like everyone else I use. Prove your loyalty and reliability."

"And what exactly makes you think I want to be a part of some low life's little underworld team?" Cole was now pushing. He was curious to see what Wayne really had to offer. Cole could tell the man had access to information on what was going down on the street.

But how far do those lines go? How dirty does it get? Cole was wondering, when Wayne spoke softly his reply, "Blood. I can promise you blood."

Wayne wasn't even sure why he said it. But, something in Cole's eyes told him that more than any amount of money he could offer, it was blood that he really wanted. "And, I can offer you the chance of spilling a whole lot more of the kind that you've been spilling lately." Wayne was still unsure of Cole's true motivations, but he took a shot and had made a guess that would either prove to be enough, or it wouldn't.

Cole studied him for a long time, weighing the pros and cons of taking this path, before responding. "What do you have in mind?" Cole asked. His body pitched forward slightly towards Wayne.

The subtle body language told Wayne he had guessed correctly. For whatever reason, it didn't really matter to Wayne, Cole was motivated truly by one thing. Spilling blood. Armed with this knowledge, Wayne quickly shifted into his comfortable position of information specialist. Providing the right people with certain information and letting them go was how it always worked. Like starting a game of pinball, all he had to do was pull the spring back and shoot the ball out in the right direction with enough force. Then the balls would do the rest of the work themselves with a little gentle coaxing here and there. This system had already worked for Wayne quite well for many years.

"Let me tell you what I've got in mind…" and Wayne leaned forward to explain what ultimately became Cole's first job with Wayne. Wayne was smart to have Cole go after a drug dealer on that first job. Cole liked the damage he could do with Wayne's information, and Wayne was right, they did work well together.

Eventually, Cole's bloodlust cooled, and Wayne decided to use Cole's talents for more sophisticated jobs. Wayne soon realized the vigilante-like tendencies that possessed Cole and planned to twist and use them for his own devices, and he did, very successfully. Wayne used Cole to take out any competition that Wayne ever came across. The problem was Cole always operated under his own strict set of morals, and

Wayne sometimes became frustrated by this. Always having to justify that the people they were dealing with were some really bad people and the world was probably going to be a better place without them in it.

Cole's life went on like this and, within a year of working for Wayne, Cole had made himself indispensable to the fat gangster. Cole was a born leader and skilled tactician who could coordinate, plan and revise a job as things changed and developed on the ground. These talents were what had kept him alive in Wayne's dangerous business for so long.

This meant nothing to Cole and, like a shark, he kept moving forward, never looking backwards at the past. He didn't want to forget his past. He would never forget Shelby. For Cole, it was too painful to have certain thoughts. Thoughts that would not heal.

Enough time had passed since Shelby's murder that Cole was no longer controlled by revenge. However, he had become a different person and his life moved too fast for him to stop and really reflect on what to do next. Cole didn't necessarily like what he had become, but he was good at it.

With his desire for retribution gone, Cole's motivation and actions had now shifted to somewhere else. A place without purpose and for the first time in his life, Cole found himself lost and without a sense of direction.

That was around the time Fragile found him and the first duplicate had tried to kill him...

CHAPTER 9
THROUGH THE LOOKING GLASS

"Where is my money, Fragile?" Wayne shouted at the older man. All signs of the pleasant and jovial fat man from the initial meeting were gone.

Fragile had called Wayne on the drive back to the safe house explaining that things had changed the crew's planned exit from the bank, but everything was fine. The other three should be right behind him in the van with the money. Not liking deviations to his plans, Wayne was already there by the time the old man arrived with the still unconscious Shane. But now, it was over an hour later and the others still hadn't arrived with the money, and Wayne could smell something was not right.

Fragile, being a much more intelligent man than Wayne, had begun to suspect after only fifteen minutes had passed without their return that something was definitely wrong. Fragile imagined the temptation of so much money was too much for Trent and Manny to resist.

But could they be stupid enough to try something? Fragile wondered idly to himself.

Meanwhile, Wayne paced nervously around the room, as his large bodyguard watched silently by the door.

"How could you be so stupid as to trust those goons with all the money? And what the hell happened to Cole?" Wayne looked at the still unconscious Shane and wondered what was wrong with him.

"Those 'goons' were hired by you, not me. I did my job and I thought Cole looked bad and might have needed medical attention." Fragile was not accustomed to defending himself, and didn't appreciate Wayne's accusatory tone.

However, his real attention and focus were back at the bank. Fragile reviewed what had happened in those last minutes before the explosion for what felt like the thousandth time. Everything had occurred so quickly, however, the old man couldn't be certain of anything. He too hoped Cole would wake up soon and provide some answers.

The doctor, whom Wayne had on standby in case something went wrong, finished bandaging Shane up and suturing a cut on his left hand. With that complete the doctor informed them that Cole should be fine. A small gash on his head and hand but nothing serious, "Cole is probably unconscious from the concussion and trauma of the grenade blast," the doctor reassured them and that he should be waking up any time now. "We could expedite the process with some smelling salts," the doctor suggested, "but it is usually better to let the patient wake up naturally." He quickly added.

Wayne said, "Do it. We need him sooner rather than later. Cole is good at handling these sorts of situations. What am I saying? He's good at handling every situation."

Fragile, for the first time, could see how much Wayne had come to rely on Cole. No longer did

Wayne look like his usual confident and pompous self, in control and manipulating everyone and everything to his will. Fragile pondered this, while he watched Wayne nervously hover around the doctor and Cole. Wayne actually sounded like he needed Cole to wake up in order to take control of the situation.

"Ughh… my head hurts. What happened?" Shane asked. He was awakened as soon as the salts were placed under his nose, and he would have been hard pressed to verbalize what he experienced.

How do you describe the sensation of an impossibility? What it would be like to travel upon two roads at once? How can I be two things occupying the same place at the same time? He asked himself.

While he was unconscious, his dreams were filled with the memories of this other person, Cole. As if he had somehow absorbed or downloaded Cole's past into his own mind. Shane could not only remember the memories, but also feel them. They vibrated and coursed through him now. A whole set of parallel memories were now riding along side his own. Minute by minute, these memories were becoming more vivid, more indistinguishable from his own. Shane's mind jealously fought for attention, working to preserve his personal identity from the intrusion by Cole.

It felt like there was a war for dominance going on inside his mind and he was losing. Unfortunately for Shane, while his mind played out its inner turmoil, what he saw wasn't making much sense to him either. Shane had awoken to find himself in some kind of warehouse.

Where the hell am I? Shane had little time to question this however because an angry fat man in a wrinkled suit was waving a smelling stick under his nose, cursing at him about missing money.

Behind the sweaty red-faced guy was a smaller man, busy placing medical equipment inside what looked to Shane like an old-fashioned physicians' bag. He could tell there were two other men there, standing outside of his periphery vision. If he didn't know better, Shane would have sworn he was watching a gangster movie. Something violent and brutal like a Scorsese or Tarantino film. Except this was a lot scarier, and they were so close to him, hovering, it made Shane feel claustrophobic.

Wayne, the apparent boss, was certain that he was this guy named Cole. Along with some of Cole's memories slowly filtering in for assistance, Shane quickly figured out these guys were killers. A strong sense of self-preservation told him that if they found out he wasn't Cole, they would kill him. Perhaps for wasting their time, let alone being a witness who could identify them and their hideout.

But, as bizarre as it was, somehow he was Cole. He couldn't explain it, but the memories of this other man's life were flooding into his mind. Memories that began over a decade ago, but before that… nothing.

For the last hour, he played it cool, acting semi-conscious, barely speaking while trying to figure out what to do next and not get himself killed. Without knowing exactly how or why he knew the fat guy was Wayne and the crippled guy was Fragile, but knowing is entirely different from believing or trusting what insanity must be going on inside his mind.

The bodyguard in the room was only relevant when the time came for them to kill him, so Shane didn't bother with him. Shane also began remembering that some guys named Trent, Manny and Jeff had made off with some money. All the while, he kept reminding himself he was supposed to be Cole.

Great! You know the names of the whole gang. Now what? Shane knew time was running out for him. He needed to somehow escape, but had no clue as to how he was going to do that.

"Cole, what happened in there? This job was supposed to go smooth and simple. What part of smooth and simple means blowing up half the damn building? Where are Trent, Manny and Jeff and, most importantly, where is my money!?" Wayne was starting to really panic.

Something was wrong with Cole. For the last hour since he woke up, he kind of sat there, listening but not saying much, and Wayne was really beginning to lose patience with Cole's silent act. "For christ's sake, speak, dammit! Or are you going to sit there like a schmuck all day?"

"I think perhaps the young man took more of a blow to the head than we might have thought." Fragile interrupted, before Wayne could fly into yet another of his tirades. "This incessant questioning of him is getting us nowhere. In addition, if it were me, I would need to get my bearings a little, you know, to think things through a bit on my own. Perhaps we should let him get changed and cleaned up? Maybe after a splash of water on his face, he'll come back to us with a plan like Cole always does. Help us figure out a way for us to find Trent and Manny and get the money back."

"Yeah, maybe you're right. Is that what you need, Cole? A little time to think? Christ, I need a drink or something anyway." Wayne gestured with his hand towards a back room, "Well, go get your stuff and take some time. Let's say in a couple of hours. I'll be back and you'll have a plan on how to get our money from those snakes, Trent and Manny. Right?"

"Sure," was all Shane could timidly reply.

Without another word and still disgusted, Wayne walked out of the safe house followed by his body-guard.

"So, *Cole*, shall we go collect our things?" The old cripple said to Shane, eyeing him closely, after Wayne had left.

'Fragile', Shane thought he had heard Wayne call the guy, and yet, somehow, he already knew that. His new memories were proving themselves to be trust-worthy, but still holding a certain degree of doubt and skepticism with them, Shane tested the name, "Hey, uh, Fragile?"

"Yes?" Fragile responded as the two of them walked into the back room where a row of lockers stood.

I better ask this guy something good. He seems a lot smart-er than that Wayne guy.

"You really think those other guys had the guts to steal the money?" Shane thought it sounded like something tough to say and, besides, he might learn some useful information from Fragile's answer.

"Trent and Manny might be stupid enough to try to steal it. I wouldn't put anything past those two, especially Trent, but I don't think the other kid was involved. In fact, I would say there is a good chance his body is floating face down somewhere right now." Shane noticed the note of sadness in Fragile's voice when he said this. Fragile was a man who didn't like senseless violence.

"The 'kid'? You mean Jeff?" Shane asked.

"Who do you think I would be referring to?" Fragile looked puzzled by Shane's behavior and questions. Cole was usually a bit quicker on the uptake. He was really acting out of it. Fragile continued anyway, "I think poor Jeff got caught up in Trent and Manny's scheme to rip us off."

Now, they were at the lockers and Shane thought he didn't know which one he should be opening. But then, from somewhere in the back of his mind, Shane knew which locker was Cole's. Without hesitation he opened it.

In the locker, Shane found a change of clothes, a cell phone and a set of keys, along with a roll of cash but no wallet or ID. He also found a coat with a large knife hidden inside one of its pockets that Fragile and the others must not have known about. Shane decided it was a good idea to keep that discovery to himself. He changed into the fresh pair of clothes, his own having been reduced to rags from the explosion in the bank, and as he did so, he noticed Fragile eyeing him carefully.

"What?" Shane asked innocently.

Fragile stood there a moment before speaking, carefully watching him. When Fragile had first seen Shane in the bank, he had simply dismissed him as Cole. After all, the odds that one of Cole's duplicates happened to be at the bank job seemed too unlikely at the time. But, something was definitely not right with Cole.

After all of this time, could it be that Cole was not the P.R.I.M.E.? Fragile wondered to himself. Making up his mind, the old man asked with a slight chuckle in his voice, "How long do you think you can keep this act up?"

"Keep what up?" Shane tried not to panic at this point.

"I don't know what is going on, but what I do know is you are not acting like Cole and, therefore, I say you most likely are not Cole. So, I am only going to say this once." Fragile spoke seriously now, "If you hope to get out of this alive, you better start doing a better job pretending to be him. Wayne has known Cole for a very long time. If I can tell the difference, there is a good chance that, eventually, so will Wayne. You're very lucky he is panicking about the money and has grown so dependent over the past couple years on Cole to solve his problems for him. I think it has blinded him to the obvious fact that you, young man, are definitely not Cole." Then, at that last bit, Fragile chuckled again to himself.

"I don't know what you're talking about, you

stupid old man." Shane said, trying to sound confident. A feeling that was usually foreign to him and yet now, oddly, somehow it wasn't.

"That's much better," Fragile said with a wink.

If the old man suspects I am not Cole, then why is he helping me? Shane wondered, as he changed into fresh clothes that were not his, yet fit perfectly.

Shane didn't realize Fragile was always extra perceptive to the way people acted and behaved. He would notice the minutest mannerisms of the people he worked with, and that had always been one of his biggest assets. In many ways, it was what had kept an old cripple like Fragile alive for so long. His attention to the details had become all the more heightened in order to identify and locate his legacy of long ago, the P.R.I.M.E. and his duplicates.

Shane had finished changing his clothes and was staring at Cole's phone, his own having been destroyed in the explosion, like it too was going to blow up in his hands at any second. From the instant Shane had woken up, he had been preoccupied with surviving the next moment and coping with the fact that Cole's life was now intertwined with and embedding itself in his own. Shane worried that, even though he had survived that explosion at the bank, he may be going completely insane.

His mind drifted towards sad thoughts of Cole's past. Memories of parents he loved but had never met. Shane suddenly felt an old, but still searing hot, anger course through him. A burning hatred and desire for revenge towards the long dead killers and destroyers of Cole's once happy family. Cole was inside of him, battling to take control of Shane, who was certain he must be losing his mind.

I have to get out of here! Shane's will was fighting for dominance within him again.

Shane turned the phone on but stopped, suddenly realizing that there was no one he could call for help or who would believe what he told them anyway.

What could I possibly say to explain the situation? "Hi there. I somehow got involved in a bank robbery and seemed to have absorbed another man along with his memories. He's the bank robber who tried to murder me, and oh yeah, he happens to look identical to me."

Yeah, they won't hang up, thinking a lunatic had called them. Not a chance. I am so screwed. Shane lamented his situation. Once again, fear was preventing him from making a decision, even when his own life was in danger.

It was Fragile who made the decision for him by pulling a gun out and pointing it at him. "Whatever it is you are thinking, whoever you are thinking of calling, I would really reconsider the decision right now, if I were you. You and I need to focus. We have a job to do right now." Fragile gestured with the barrel of the gun for Shane to put the cell phone back into the locker.

"I wasn't going to call the cops or anything. I wanted to call… oh, never mind," Shane stopped, understanding Fragile's point.

It didn't matter whom he called or if they believed him or not. Any communication could bring the authorities down on them and Fragile wasn't going to allow it. Shane reluctantly put the phone back in Cole's locker.

Should have pocketed the phone along with that knife in the coat. I'm such an idiot. Shane chastised himself. He was after all rather new to all of this.

"Let's both agree it would be best if we focus on the task at hand. Wayne is going to be back here faster than you think. Have you come up with a plan yet to find our money? Or are you too preoccupied with Cole's mobile phone to–" Fragile stopped mid-sentence, his eyes fixed on the phone sitting in Cole's locker.

A smile leaped across the old man's face, as he remembered something Jeff had told him earlier that day. They could track down and locate Jeff's laptop using his phone. But they had to hurry. Jeff needed their help, and Trent and Manny were getting further away with every passing minute with the money and, more importantly for Fragile and Cole, the envelope that was still hidden within it.

"So...Cole–" Fragile intentionally exaggerated the name for effect, "you know anything about smart phones and GPS devices?" As he asked the question, Fragile opened up another locker, Jeff's, pulled out a smartphone and held it towards Shane.

"Sure, of course," Shane replied.

"Well, take a look at this and see if you can find anything on there that looks like it can locate a missing computer?" Fragile was excited. This was the best opportunity they were going to have at getting back that envelope and their money, but they had to move quick-ly. Odds were that Trent and Manny would dump Jeff, the van and anything else that could be tracked down.

"What is this? I mean whose phone is this?" Shane asked while the phone powered on.

"It was Jeff's, and before we went out to do the job this morning, he mentioned to me that this device could locate and erase the information on his com-puter, the one that he had with him the last time I saw him," Fragile said.

Shane searched through the phone's applications and soon found the program he was looking for. Al-most immediately, a map screen came into view with a blinking pin that was moving down a street. When he tapped the pin with his finger, it indicated the location in detail along with the directions to the other side of town from Shane and Fragile's current location.

"Fragile, you better take a look at this. I think I found it," Shane said.

Fragile looked at the location on the smart phone Shane was holding and said, "We better move fast, if we wish to retain any hope of finding them." Fragile made a signal to leave.

"Aren't we going to wait for Wayne? I mean…" Shane corrected himself, "Won't Wayne get suspicious if we are gone when he gets back?" *Confidence. Play the role of Cole or you're dead.* Shane told himself.

"Oh, for God sakes, would you please drop that act with me already? Save it for Wayne. Here, you're going to need this," Fragile handed Shane back Cole's cell phone. He wasn't sure what was going on, but for the time being at least, Fragile wanted Shane to continue playing the part of Cole, at least as far as Wayne was concerned. Fragile would have to find out more regarding this new duplicate later.

"You might want to do a better job with that act, if Wayne happens to come around."

"You mean we're going after them… after Trent and Manny? Just the two of us?" Shane asked but stood, almost reflexively. "Suppose we find them? Then, what?"

"As my mum used to say, 'We'll burn that bridge when we get to it,' meaning first things first." Fragile headed towards the door. "Now, we really must be going, and I am going to need your assistance. Heavy lifting and all." Fragile joked as he walked towards the door.

Shane stood there unsure, as he often did, of what to do next. But, a voice in his head sounding much like his own and yet somehow different commanded him to act.

Cole's more confident voice, said, *Go!*

Shane headed for the door, immediately after he grabbed the coat with Cole's knife in it.

CHAPTER 10
BREADCRUMBS

They had been following Jeff's GPS laptop tracker all across town. Shane was sitting in the passenger's seat of Fragile's car. He was studying Jeff's smartphone running the application that was tracking the computer along with Jeff and the money. However, finding the computer also meant finding those two psychopaths from the bank.

Shane could still remember how callously they had killed in the bank. The huge guy, Manny, had snapped the bank guard's neck with ease and that little weasely looking guy, Trent killed those two tellers and who knows how many more with that explosion.

"They've definitely stopped moving," he said to Fragile, as the old man drove according to the coordinates Shane had given him. "Based on what this device says, the van has been parked in the same spot for the last thirty minutes–looks like they've stopped moving." Shane guessed.

Fragile remained silent, like he had for the majority of the drive. Fragile's mind raced as fast as the vehicle under his control. When he did speak to Shane, it was for further directions from the GPS unit.

Maybe he is working on the plan for if and when we catch up with Trent and Manny? Shane wondered. *Well, he'd better have a good plan, because those psychopaths looked like they could handle a small army, let alone an old cripple and a book-*

store manager.

"So, we're going to follow them?" Shane asked, trying to keep the doubt from creeping into his voice.

Fragile's hands loosened on the steering wheel, and he looked over at Shane. They were too close to abandon the mission now. Fragile knew the envelope contained what he and Cole had searched so long for, and they may never get an opportunity like this again. Like the initial bank job itself, going after Trent and Manny to recover that envelope was worth the risks. After a deep exhale, Fragile had made up his mind and was now resolved to see it through till the end.

"Yes. We are going to follow them," Fragile responded, "Then, we are going to get Jeff, and the money. And, you're going to try to stay alive through it all, aren't you, Cole?" Fragile winked at Shane.

This is going to be an interesting afternoon. Shane adjusted in his seat and prepared himself for the car ride that was going to take him directly towards two killers, their hostage, and a van filled with millions in stolen bank money.

— — — — —

Shane and Fragile were a few blocks away from where the signal had come to stop over an hour ago.

"We're getting close, Fragile," Shane said quietly, "You have a plan on this, or are we going to go in guns blazing like an Old Western?"

"I have an idea," was all the old man said in reply.

Great. Now the guy has turned into a silent Clint East-wood type. Monosyllabic and mysterious. Shane was seriously concerned about confronting these killers alone. He had seen Trent and Manny kill people without remorse or hesitation. He didn't know what Fragile's plan was, but if it involved only the two of them, Shane had serious doubts about it.

The GPS locator had taken them across town to a large public storage facility. The gate required a code to get in, so Fragile and Shane waited outside the entrance, until another car came along a couple of minutes later and followed it in. They made two left turns and one right turn, as they navigated the labyrinth style public storage maze, until they were outside a larger unit that was used for RV and Boat storage. The GPS pin on the screen Shane was holding indicated that the laptop was inside unit number 221B.

Fragile had popped the trunk and was exiting the vehicle, before Shane had even unfastened his seatbelt.

For an old crippled guy, he sure does move fast when he wants to. Shane thought as he got out of the car.

Fragile was standing by the trunk waiting for Shane, "I will need your assistance for this, and we will need to move quickly, so if you can keep the questions to a minimum." Fragile was all business now, as he pulled the gun out of his jacket.

"Are they in there hiding out or something?" Shane asked, not wanting to be involved in a gun battle.

"I highly doubt it. I suspect those two dumped the van and the money here, while they decided where to go and what to do next. From what I know regarding these two, they probably only took enough money with them as they needed to get a room to hole up in, and figure things out. Violent morons of this type usually only think a couple of moves ahead anyway, but we still shouldn't take any chances, so let's be quick about it," Fragile directed Shane to pick up a pair of giant bolt clippers from a tool bag he had inside his trunk. "We're going to need that."

Shane had the padlock off and the door rolled up within the next minute. The storage unit was dark inside. The late afternoon sun was not shedding much light into the space, casting deep shadows. Shane could barely make out the lone shape of a van parked inside. He opted to let Fragile move deeper into the unit and have a look inside the van.

Fragile saw what he had half expected to find. Easily visible from the side passenger door was the corpse of Jeff, the young computer hacker, a single bullet between his open eyes, and surrounded by six bags of stolen bank money.

"I'm truly sorry young man," was all Fragile said.

Jeff looked like he had made it, until the van was parked inside the storage unit, before meeting with the working end of either Manny or Trent's gun. Fragile flipped on the unit's light, illumining it in a bright yellow hue.

"Is that kid dead?" Shane asked, coming in trying to get a look past Fragile.

"Yes... Yes he is. Now come on, mate," Fragile sighed deeply, "Let's get this over with." Fragile indicated that Shane should hand over the bolt cutters and with one good swing of his good arm, Fragile smashed the passenger window, reached in and unlocked the van.

"But, what if Trent and Manny come back?" Shane worried.

"Then, we had better get this done, and leave before they do, don't you think?" Fragile had slid the side door open and grabbed one of the enormous bags full of cash, unzipped it and rifled through its contents. He was desperately searching for the envelope that had to be hidden somewhere within one of them.

After searching a second bag and then a third and finding nothing, Fragile's search became increasingly frantic. His job was all the more desperate now without Cole's help. After the sixth and final bag had been searched and no envelope found, Fragile was in a full panic.

"There was an envelope in one of these bags. We need to locate that envelope! No matter what," Fragile said this mostly to himself.

"What's the big deal? We got the money back for that Wayne guy, and besides, with all of this money we can—" Shane was saying.

"If you remember, Cole," Fragile made sure to exaggerate the name, "the money was not why you and I were doing this job..." Fragile did not elaborate, before lugging one of the bags into the trunk of his sedan.

Shane really didn't need more prompting than that and grabbed two of the bank bags himself and threw them in Fragile's open trunk.

"I don't get it. Even with this envelope missing, why would they leave all this cash here like this? Isn't that a little stupid?" Shane asked.

"What were they supposed to do with it?" Fragile questioned. "It's not like they can carry it around with them without attracting a lot of attention. In addition, I don't think Trent or Manny are the smartest men you'll ever meet. Their strengths lie in their brutality and willingness to kill anyone. Their plan probably didn't extend much further than laying low in a crowded city, while they figured out what to do next."

When they had finished loading the car with the money, Fragile grabbed Jeff's laptop and handed it to Shane. "Here, see if you can find out anything on this. Maybe Jeff used it to book them hotel rooms? Otherwise, we're going to have to stake this place out and wait for them to come back for the money."

"But, we got the money…Shouldn't we just leave and consider ourselves lucky we got away without a fight?" Shane seriously doubted any good would come from confronting Trent and Manny, especially once they found out they no longer had possession of the money.

"If we don't deal with this now, the problem will follow us home." Fragile pointed at the poor dead computer nerd in the back of the van to emphasize his point. "Do you want to end up like Jeff, or worse?" Fragile asked, as he got back behind the wheel of his car.

The old man had a point. Shane rubbed his eyes,

looking up at the afternoon sun, which was now lowering itself behind the storage facility building. Then, abruptly, he closed the rolling door of the storage unit and got in the passenger seat.

As they left the facility, Shane put on his seatbelt and toggled the keypad on Jeff's laptop computer.

"Can we please get some coffee before anything else?" Shane half begged, his exhaustion from the day starting to catch up with him.

"I think we can do that," Fragile said, smiling now for the first time in hours.

As it turned out, Jeff's computer was still on and had been left in sleep mode. They must have killed Jeff, before he had a chance to power down the machine. A lucky break for Fragile and Shane too, because the odds were good that Jeff would have had a password on the computer if they'd had to turn the machine back on.

That was the good news…

The bad news was what the open window on the screen displayed.

Two photos were visible. Obviously taken from the bank's video surveillance camera earlier, one was of Shane standing by the teller line. The other was of Cole. There was little doubt that the two men looked identical but were not the same person.

If Trent and Manny knew about me, then maybe they could even find out where I live. Shane thought trying hard not to panic.

"They saw a bank photo of me and Cole. If they find out who I am… Fragile, they could find me."

Shane, in full panic now, didn't care if the old guy knew he wasn't Cole.

"Try to stay calm and find out where they are staying for the night," Fragile reassured Shane. "We will take care of them, before anything bad happens. I promise."

Shane found what Fragile had wanted within minutes. The computer had its internet browser still on. Where they got their coffees, Shane used the shop's free WiFi to refresh the page and view the last thing Jeff had done on the computer before he died. The page refreshed to reveal Jeff's email inbox with the newest unopened mail, a confirmation of his purchase of two connecting suites at a nearby hotel.

"We got them," Shane said, while sipping his coffee. "They're at the Remington Hotel on Main Street."

"They had a couple hours head start on us. Let's wait a while longer and let them enjoy their new wealth for a while. Let the alcohol, drugs do their work, and then, we'll go finish this when they're sleeping it off."

"You mean kill them!?" Shane was not ready to go to that next level.

"How did you think this had to end?" Fragile asked Shane. "Do you really think people like Trent and Manny will simply go away? They have nothing to lose. Once they find out they don't have the money anymore, these guys will hunt you down and slit your throat while you sleep."

"But, I'm not a killer, Fragile," Shane said plainly, dropping all pretense of acting like Cole. "You know I'm not him… this guy Cole. You knew it while we were still back at the safe house, and yet you still brought me along all this way. Why?"

"I brought you with me, because I had a better chance of doing this my way, if Wayne wasn't involved. But, I still need Cole for my plan to work. All I need you to do when the time comes is to not say a word. Just stand there and try to look like Cole. Maybe nod your head when I tell you to. Don't worry, neither you nor I will have to get our hands dirty." Fragile explained in a calm voice, "Which reminds me, may I see Cole's phone? I need to call some of his old friends out in this area."

– – – – –

When considering any act of violence, it is important to remember that random acts are much more difficult to trace. Fragile's plan for dealing with Trent and Manny definitely involved a high degree of violence. Thus, he planned to utilize the services of professionals who could quickly be contacted, negotiated with, and the job rendered with a large amount of respect for anonymity.

After making the call and driving to the decided meeting place, Fragile and Shane now found themselves in a back alley meeting with these so-called 'professionals'.

Biker-gangs, like the Hell's Angels, always traveled in large groups. Shane counted at least eight, maybe more.

Fragile turned towards Shane, "Now, I'm not sure how many of these guys know Cole or how well. I do know that the leader, that guy right there in the middle with the red and white bandana on his head, knows Cole real well, so he's the one you're going to have to convince. His name is Chris Brewer, but his friends call him 'Chuppa.'"

Shane wasn't even convinced himself, "I don't think I can do this. Isn't there another way? I think you should know Fragile, that I hate your plan already!"

"No, there is not another way. Not without dealing with Trent and Manny ourselves, and am I correct in saying that is something neither of us really want to do? Now, just relax. Don't forget how much you and Cole look alike. Don't say too much, and you'll be fine." Fragile assured him, before stepping out of the car and walking into the dark alleyway where the bikers were impatiently waiting.

Shane cursed under his breath, got out of the car and tried to imagine what Cole would look like walking up to fierce looking Hell's Angels. Confident and fearless, no doubt. The two traits Shane had pretty much always lacked.

"Hey, Cole, good times! It has been a stretch, bro," Chuppa called to his old friend.

"Hey," was all Shane could croak out, before his mouth went very dry.

Fragile jumped in at this point, "Cole's not feeling so well right now. He's been under a lot of strain lately. Wayne's been working him endlessly, which is actually why we contacted you for help." Fragile went on, "Two of Wayne's guys have gone rogue. Stole some money and an envelope. We've recovered the money, but the envelope has gone missing. Wayne authorized a compensation that I believe will more than make up for the short notice and the seriousness of the work." Fragile handed Chuppa a small duffle bag full of cash. Two hundred thousand dollars.

"You'll get another bag like that one, after you've done the job, with a bonus if you recover the envelope that went missing along with them." Fragile added.

After looking inside the bag and giving it a rough count, Chuppa's eyes revealed a look of reverent giddiness at all that cash. That look however, was quickly replaced by a wiser street sense when he replied flatly, "We're not interested. This kind of money is only paid for whacking somebody."

"Two somebody's actually. With a bonus if you recover the envelope." Fragile put in.

Chuppa turned to Shane, "Cole, man, you know we've been trying to stay away from this kinda thing, ever since that shit went down at the casino in Vegas a few years ago. A lot of brothers are still doing time for that one." Chuppa felt uncomfortable and eyed his crew with a look that said, *It's not worth it. Let's go.*

It's now or never, Shane thought and drew himself up confidently. "Chuppa, I wouldn't ask you for this, if I didn't need the help." Then, he added, "Plus, I'll personally double the money for you and your brothers on the back end, if you find my envelope."

Fragile looked sharply at Shane, but Shane ignored him. If he was to act confidently, the way Cole would, then screw Fragile, his money and his stupid mystery envelope.

"You know it's not the money, bro. The only reason I'd even consider it is because I owe you, man. Big time." Chuppa stared at Shane closely, making a decision.

Oh no! Why is he looking at me like that? Shane panicked.

But, Chuppa had already made up his mind, "Alright. Let's do this. Now, who are the two lucky bastards? I am so excited to meet them," Chuppa's smile was menacing.

By the look on his face and the way he said this, Shane was certain Chuppa was a very dangerous man.

Fragile turned to Shane and said, "Brilliant! Brilliant, Cole, we better be going. Now." Fragile spoke over his shoulder, "Chuppa, we'll call you with the details of the job in the next five minutes. After the work is done, I'll tell you how to get the rest of your money. And, Chuppa, don't underestimate these two," Fragile said, referring to Trent and Manny, "They're some mean hombres, if you know what I'm saying," Fragile warned the biker.

"Yeah, well, we're a couple of regular boy-scouts here ourselves. Ain't that right, boys?"

Shane could hear the rest of Chuppa's crew laugh at this joke as he and Fragile got back into their car. The hostility that exuded from these men almost made Shane feel a little sorry for Trent and Manny.

- - - - -

Shane stared out of the window silently, while Fragile drove the car along the highway. It was late afternoon, and the sun was casting its final salmon colored rays across the horizon.

Shane and Fragile were on their way back to the safe house. Except for the poor dead guy, Jeff, and the missing envelope, they had accomplished what they had set out to do. They recovered the money for Wayne and dealt with Trent and Manny.

"Fragile, I need to go home," Shane said, completely exhausted.

"I know. We need to take care of this," Fragile gestured with his head towards the trunk filled with the six large duffle bags of cash.

Shane was beginning to panic, "I don't care about the money. I don't even care that I might be going completely insane. I just want out. I'm done with all of this."

"Wayne needs to be assured that he's going to receive his money and that there are no witnesses to implicate him," Fragile made sure to emphasize this last part so that Shane would fully understand the situation they were in.

"If Wayne finds out who I really am, that I'm not Cole, you think he might go after me? After my mom?" Shane shuddered at this last thought.

"There is more going on than I can explain right now, but know that Wayne is the least of our problems. We need to keep all of this as quiet as possible until you can make the full fusion with Cole and the other duplicates he's absorbed. If the Director finds out about you we will have no time. So like I said earlier, bringing in this money is going to keep both of us alive, but it will require that we each handle things very carefully," was Fragile's only answer.

Shane sat quietly, resigning himself to the fact that one way or another he was going to have to see this thing through until the end. If nothing else but for his mom's safety.

"What difference does it make? Now that you've been found, the odds of you being alive this time next week is slim to none anyway. Dammit, we needed to intercept that envelope!" Fragile's own patience with the whole affair was at an end.

Shane stared at the old man intently for a while, before saying, "You know more than you're letting on, don't you, Fragile? What do you mean I most likely won't be alive next week?"

Fragile drove for a time before answering, "I was a much younger man when this all began. I thought I could handle the responsibility. That I was smart enough to take care of it all by myself, but I was wrong... I was arrogant and cocky and it split you up. Fragmented you and now I've been picking up the pieces ever since." Fragile momentarily fell silent, briefly lost in the past before continuing, "Years ago, I was among the world's top neuro-geneticists. That's when the Cabal enlisted me into the program and I was placed under Director Gray. Without sounding too self-congratulatory, Director Gray knew if anyone could figure out a way to do it, I could. Gray had enlisted, kidnapped or whatever else some of the greatest minds at that time. Told us we would change the world for the better. Cure cancer and other diseases. Give people a chance to live even longer, healthier lives. Who wouldn't want to be a part of something like that?" He laughed at the irony of it all. "We didn't think it was all for them and that they never planned or intended on sharing it with the rest of the world."

"Do what Fragile? What did you do?" Shane asked, breaking the old man out of his private reverie.

"The Cabal wanted to live forever." Fragile looked old when he answered, "Even with all of the money and power in the world it wasn't enough for them. They want to keep it forever, as if they could." Fragile chuckled when he said, "Some people are so poor that all they have is money." His mind was somewhere in the past. "The long ago failed experiment that created the P.R.I.M.E.," Fragile explained, "was nothing more than the age old search for eternal life. The members of the Cabal want to live forever. They wanted us to create the Fountain of Youth."

"Tell me Fragile." Scared as he was, Shane knew he had to hear this, "Tell me everything."

— — — — —

"The team of scientists they had assembled had made little progress for years and I was the one who was supposed to somehow circumvent all of that." Fragile chuckled to himself before he began to recount the story as he drove.

"Biological aging is really nothing more than

an aging cell's inability to create perfect duplications of itself. Over time our bodies are corrupted through toxins and free radicals that overwhelm and corrupt the process. My idea was to induce what is known as neurogenesis and neuroplasticity."

"What is that?" asked Shane, fascinated by these concepts he had never heard of before.

"Neurogenesis is when brain cells are created. This process occurs while a baby is forming in the mother's womb. Neuroplasticity allows your brain to create new brain cells and connections."

"So, those two things are literally what happens to you while your brain is forming in utero." Shane understood what Fragile was saying thus far and urged the old man to continue.

"Correct," Fragile was pleased at how fast the kid caught on, "My idea was that if we created a modified genetic structure that would perform perfect cellular duplication indefinitely, we could halt the aging process. This way all of the cell types remained pluripotent cells and would act and perform like embryonic stem cells." Fragile's mind, perhaps out of habit, was racing towards his idea's logical conclusion. Even now after all of these years, the theory still seemed sound to the old scientist.

"And like embryonic stem cells they could become any kind of cell that is needed to continue the process towards perfect cellular replication." Shane finished for him, following Fragile's line of thought. He could tell Fragile was impressed so he added, "I've had a few conversations with people, you know scientists and doctors and stuff, regarding the whole stem cell issue back when there was a political debate. I've always had a good memory." Shane shrugged as an explanation.

Fragile knew then that he was going to like this new incarnation of the P.R.I.M.E.. Shane possessed a quality that all of the previous duplicates, even Cole, had lacked. Curiosity.

"Precisely, by inducing a 'forced' expression of certain genes, we could theoretically get them to do whatever we wanted. So, for instance," Fragile added, "we excite the genes that produce the body's Fibroblast growth factor or FGF proteins. These growth factor proteins stimulated cellular growth, proliferation and cellular differentiation indefinitely. As opposed to naturally stopping as it does in adults. A little over a year later, you were born. However, rather than creating perfect duplicates of yourself on merely a cellular level, you displayed the ability to create entire replicas of yourself within the first hour of your birth. You should have seen the chaos it created. The lab looked like a nursery by the end of the day." Fragile chuckled to himself recalling the memory. "The neuroplasticity gives your brain and body the ability to change structurally and functionally as a result of input from various stimuli. In your particular case, each time you fuse and absorb one of your replicants, a complete cortical re-matting occurs. Of course, we didn't know at the time the extent in which you could reabsorb them. That you could make the duplicates at all was enough for the one in charge of the program to see you as an incredible weapon."

Shane's eyes grew wide with the realization of what was happening to him. "So… if I'm understanding you correctly–my entire brain has been reconfigured to include Cole's brain structure and cells."

"Exactly. That is how his memories and abilities have become your own." Fragile confirmed.

"But how come I absorbed him and not the other way around?" Shane asked. "What makes me P.R.I.M.E. Over all of the other duplicates I create?"

"That was precisely what we were trying to identify when Evangeline stole you from the lab." Fragile answered honestly. "We knew the process in which your abilities manifested themselves. We couldn't figure out why? But you already started to manifest abilities that could be used for terrible things if you were to fall into the wrong hands. This is precisely why Van got you out of there. But as I said earlier, in my arrogance, I made a mistake and something happened early on that split you up. Since then…I've spent all of these years trying to pick up the various pieces of you.–"

"Did Cole think he was the P.R.I.M.E?" Shane asked.

"Cole wasn't the P.R.I.M.E., and now that you have taken over, there is a process of integration in order for you to fully utilize your abilities. A neuronal fusion between your's and Cole's unique brain structures, whereby your minds will become one discreet identity. The Alpha and the Omega. The P.R.I.M.E.. I'm afraid if we don't get that envelope back you might not survive long enough to figure it out."

"Integrate what and utilize what abilities? Fragile, what does all of this have to do with me?" Shane asked.

The old man was going to answer Shane's question but was interrupted by his own phone ringing. Fragile listened and responded to the caller, "Listen, Wayne. We've got your money and are headed to you right now."

Shane's thoughts drifted with all of this new information. Like the waves lapping at the seashore, he felt his memories merging and coalescing with Cole's memories. The overlapping recollections caused Shane to believe his mind had completely cracked and this whole bizarre experience was merely the hallucinations of a paranoid schizophrenic.

Shane's mind kept trying to differentiate the new set of memories that had somehow implanted themselves into his head from his own. He had completely absorbed Cole's life in an instant, and now, he had to reconcile the other man's mind with his own. However bizarre and fantastic all this was, something told Shane that the key to getting out of this mess alive would come from understanding and gaining control over what was happening to him. Shane couldn't help but fight this new presence of Cole that was locked inside of him. He could feel Cole was there lurking and waiting for a chance to gain dominance. This was not a fusion or synthesis of two minds as Fragile had characterized it. This was an all out war for dominance. It was as if his own personal identity were at risk of being lost forever. The one odd thing Shane did notice was the sensation of feeling more whole, somehow more complete, than he had for as long as he could remember. This enigmatic perception evaded his ability to communicate nor describe the sensation.

Then suddenly, they were at Wayne's exit and Fragile pulled off the freeway. "Let's get this over with," said Fragile, and Shane thought he heard a note of doubt in the old man's voice for the first time that day.

CHAPTER 11
HOUSE GUESTS

After a few minutes' drive, they turned off onto a private road, leading up to a mansion, a virtual castle really, built into the hills. As the gate let them in, Shane and Fragile could clearly see that the lights were on inside the house.

"Looks like Wayne's waiting for us. You ready to be Cole one last time?" Fragile winked at Shane.

In answer, Shane simply shrugged. *What else can I do? Take one step in front of the next step and you'll get through this.* He kept telling himself.

They parked the car in the front next to an enormous fountain complete with cherubs pouring water from their carafes. When the car came to a stop in the enormous circular driveway, several huge men, a lot like the bodyguard who was with Wayne at the safe house, immediately surrounded them.

A guard on each side of the car opened their doors for them. Shane wasn't entirely sure if the big men, by their manner or attitude, were there to escort them or detain them.

"I'll need to open the trunk," Fragile said. "Wayne wants me to bring him the money personally."

"Do what you gotta do, man," one of the big guards spoke, "We were told to make sure it was the old cripple and the pretty-boy here." The big guard gestured towards Shane when he said this." And to make sure the money bags were brought in with you," the guard added, waving his large hand towards the trunk of Fragile's car.

"They are right here. If you would be so kind as to help us with them, we would be ever grateful. They are quite heavy, and there are six of them in all." Fragile was always the gentleman, ignoring the guard's rude comments entirely. "Cole?" Fragile went on, glancing over at Shane, "Shall we go talk to Wayne, while these men follow us with the money?"

"Uh, yeah, sure, that will be fine," Shane stumbled over his words, as he followed Fragile into the large mansion. The presence of these ominous looking men was weakening Shane's confidence. He put his hand into Cole's jacket pocket, allowing his fingers to rest on the cold metal of the large knife hidden there. Not that Shane really knew what to do with the thing, but the knife at least gave him a little assurance that he might not be totally helpless, should things turn bad in the next few minutes. Plus, Fragile was there, and he, at least so far, tried to help Shane stay alive through all of this.

Shane did not have much time to reflect on this, because before they had even reached the top of the steps, the enormous front doors swung open, and Wayne was standing there wearing an expensive black Italian suit, French cuffs and a large grin on his fat, deceivingly cherub-like face. It looked as though Wayne had cleaned up out of the wrinkled suit he had been wearing earlier and thrown a few drinks back while he was at it.

"Come on in, boys!" Wayne greeted them, perhaps a bit too enthusiastically, "Welcome to my humble abode. And I see you've brought with you the money. How glorious! How absolutely grand! You certainly turned this around from being a total and complete cluster. Well done."

"We simply finished the job you hired us to do," Fragile said cautiously.

It was obvious that Wayne was drunk. Really drunk. This apparently alarmed Fragile. Then, confirming this, Fragile turned subtly to Shane and whispered, "Don't be fooled by his cheery banter. He's a mean drunk. Watch yourself," he warned Shane.

Watch myself? Watch myself do what!? Shane had no idea what Fragile meant by a 'mean drunk.' Was that a cue not to say too much or to act a certain way? How was he supposed to know? Shane hoped Wayne himself, however, would soon provide the answers to at least some of his questions.

— — — — —

At that moment, Shane's mother, Rebecca Fisher, was getting home from work. She barely had time to put her things down and hadn't even let Bear, Shane's dog, inside from the yard, when the doorbell rang.

Who could that be? She wondered as she headed to the door.

Rebecca opened it to find a very short, rat-like man with a virtual giant standing behind him. Neither looked nice or pleasant. Rebecca only cracked the door as far as the safety latch would allow. Somehow, even that felt like too much for these two hoodlums. She noticed the smaller one was holding an envelope in his hand.

"Why hello there!" Trent said smiling, in a nasally enthusiastic voice, "We are looking for our good friend." He looked down at the envelope, as if to confirm, before saying, "Shane Fisher. Can we come in?"

"You're friends of Shane?" Rebecca asked skeptically. There was something wrong with the way the smaller man smiled, almost like he had something alive inside his mouth struggling to escape his lips. The other one, an enormous man stood there, with no trace of humor on his face.

"Forgive me. I should have introduced ourselves. My name is Trent, and this big fellow here is Emmanuel."

"Manny," Manny corrected Trent. He hated when people called him Emmanuel. It reminded him of when his mother would call him to her room, usually to punish him with a belt or paddle.

"Of course, Manny," Trent amended.

Rebecca didn't care what their names were. Something was seriously off with these two. "I'm sorry, but Shane isn't here right now. I'm not sure when he'll be back, so if you want to give him a call, I'm sure–" Rebecca apologized as she began closing the door.

Suddenly an enormous hand shot out from nowhere and blocked the door from closing.

The smaller man never stopped smiling. "I'm afraid you don't understand… we really need to speak with Shane. I'm sure it won't be a problem, if we come in for a little while to wait for him. Isn't that right, Rebecca?" Trent and Manny pushed their way through the door, snapping the chain lock easily. Any pretense of civility now gone.

If Rebecca wasn't scared before, she certainly was petrified now.

— — — — —

"Have you finally snapped out of whatever problem you were having? My god Fragile, what's the matter with him? He still looks like a freaking imbecile standing there like that." Wayne leaned in towards Shane, "What, Cole, what is it? You want to read me a book or something? For some odd reason, you look like a complete jack-ass, nerd to me right now." Wayne said, breaking Shane's proximity bubble with his stale and putrid alcohol breath.

I am so dead. I am so dead... was all Shane's mind could think. *Come on, Shane, what would a guy like Cole say?* Shane didn't even know him, but what he did know of Cole was frightening. Shane had noticed earlier that if he relaxed his own mind, more of Cole would come to the surface. All day since the bank, Shane had been fighting a private battle for dominance with Cole. But Shane was tired of this internal battle. His brain hurt from processing all of the duplicate or P.R.I.M.E. information and completely absorbing Cole. Not to mention staying alive in his bizarre and violent world. He stopped thinking about anything in particular, while he tightened his grip around the blade in his jacket. He cleared his mind of all fear. His desire to go home outweighed everything else at this point. He pictured it clearly. Being home, safe and sound was all Shane concentrated on. Exhaustion had taken its dominant hold on him at this point.

My duplicate, Cole, is some Kung Fu/special forces trained, vigilante-mafia-bank robbing-killer. Ok. I get that. Sarcastic, tired and completely pissed off. I am seriously feeling that too. So, Shane tried something new for the first time since this all happened.

He let Cole take over.

"That's probably because I'm really tired, fat man. So tired, I'm trying really hard to finish this without killing everyone in the room right now. Then maybe, I can finally get some rest. So, can we get on with it?" Shane barely recognized his own voice, let alone the words that were coming out of his mouth. Cole had spoken through him and even he could feel the danger and threat that was emanating from within him. Somewhere deep down, Shane knew he could and would kill everyone in that room, well, maybe not Fragile, but everyone else for sure. If Wayne or one of his stupid guards were to even blink in a way that offended him things were going to get very ugly. For the first time in his life, Shane felt power over brutal and vicious men. A very dangerous and violent kind of power, and to his surprise, Shane kind of liked it.

As drunk as he was, Wayne still had sense enough to flinch at this, perhaps it was a primal sense of self preservation, and backed down. Something in the way

Shane said these words made Wayne believe the old Cole, the very dangerous Cole, was back, standing before him. Even as drunk as Wayne was, he managed to remember the fact that Cole was always someone to be respected.

"Cole, of course. You know I'm only kidding? You know how I can be when I drink, ha-ha?" Wayne was all smiles now, "Silly old Wayne, playing games. Nothing serious, no offense. I am certainly grateful we could use your contacts to handle the whole Trent and Manny thing–"

"If I may interrupt," it was Fragile, "I believe what Cole is getting at, Wayne, is that we're both really tired and want our money so we can go home."

"Of course. Of course." Wayne spoke to one of his guards, standing nearest to him and said, "Please take these bags to the den. Use the money counter and divide the money out in three ways please. I will have the money wired into both of your usual offshore accounts." Wayne shrugged back at Fragile and Shane and then explained, "With Jeff, Trent and Manny gone, our cuts all increased. Not to mention, that snafu over at the bank killed our contact, the bank manager, Mr. Thomas. He won't be needing his cut either," Wayne said all this in mock sadness.

"Actually, I think Jeff's portion should be going to his mother," Fragile spoke these words with a tone that was saying that this subject was not open to debate. He confirmed this by simply adding, "It's what Jeff, 'your young friend,' would have wanted," Fragile said, eliciting Wayne's own words, from earlier that day, against him.

"Fragile, let's be sensible about this, shall we? I mean the poor kid is dead. You said so yourself. It's not going to be doing him any good, and that stripper, whore mother of his, what is she going to do with all that money?" Wayne asked the crippled old man.

"You are correct, Wayne. Money won't mean anything to her, when her son never comes home. Though perhaps, at least, it will offer a small measure of comfort that her son provided for her in the end." Fragile wasn't even sure why he felt so strongly, but he knew he wasn't going to budge on this. Not an inch.

Shane, having wrestled away and regained control from Cole again internally, now waited for the explosion from Wayne. But nothing happened. Wayne stared at Shane for a long while, perhaps measuring the risk before finally saying, "Ok, whatever… it's your call. I'm not going to go back on a deal. You know me, honest to a fault." Wayne laughed at his own joke, before he turned and left the room.

— — — — —

Less than thirty minutes later, Shane and Fragile were back in the car. For a while, the two men did not exchange a word and barely more than a glance with each other.

It was Fragile who spoke first, "I know you have a lot of questions and all of this is very confusing for you, but I assure you everything will make sense, if you give it enough time."

"Enough time? Fragile, my head feels like I'm being split into two people. Actually, scratch that twenty people. This Cole guy's memories and impulses are trying to take over, and something tells me he's only the tip of the schizophrenic iceberg," Shane said. Since he had let Cole take over at Wayne's, even briefly, Shane felt like it was an impossible struggle to regain control.

"You were never meant to have your replicants away from you for so long, so the first time you re-absorb them, it is very disorienting. Try not to fight it. I've been told, by Cole, that it speeds the process up, if you don't resist the others' memories. You won't lose yourself, I assure you. You are assumed P.R.I.M.E. You absorbed Cole, it appears, so your identity is dominant."

At first, Fragile explained, he was all but convinced that Cole had been the P.R.I.M.E.. But, the old man knew that a day would come, when Cole too would be absorbed by the Alpha replicant. The one true P.R.I.M.E.

"Nevertheless, Cole came with plenty of useful tools and tricks of his own to track down and find more duplicates than I could have imagined."

"What the hell is a Prime anyway?" Shane asked incredulously.

"The P.R.I.M.E.: or Primary, Replicating, Initial, Material, Example, is what we called the first test subject, well, the first test subject that survived anyway," Fragile said sheepishly. "The P.R.I.M.E. was number one… the first being we created. You now are the numerical Alpha in the apparent chronological and biological hierarchy that governs the entire re-absorption process," Fragile saw none of this was getting through to Shane, so he tried a different approach. "In other words, the P.R.I.M.E. always wins. The P.R.I.M.E. will always absorb and mentally dominate when confronted with one of its replicants. Over the past years, I have been able to watch and test, especially with Cole, the various incredible abilities that you possessed, and would gain with each new duplicate," Fragile looked over at Shane, "first as a child and now as a young man." The old man said this last with a fatherly tone in his voice.

"It sure doesn't feel like it. Well, I am glad I survived long enough to justify formally making your acquaintance, Fragile," Shane's voice dripped with sarcasm.

"All I can say is, in the past, you usually would fully integrate your long term replicants within a week or two. All of their memories, skill-sets and abilities that Cole had acquired over the years will soon be yours." Fragile looked over, as if for the first time all day, and asked, "So– now that you actually survived the day, what is your name, son?"

"Shane. My name is Shane Fisher."

"Jewish?" Fragile asked the newest P.R.I.M.E..

"Yes, I am. Why? Is there something wrong with that?" Shane tried his best to keep a defensive tone out of his voice.

"Something wrong? No son," The old man chuckled at this question. "There is absolutely nothing wrong with you being Jewish. I just find it very interesting is all." Fragile didn't elaborate any further than that. Silence prevailed in the car for an awkward moment or two.

"What's yours? It couldn't really be Fragile. No parent is that cruel," Shane joked, nervously attempting to change the subject.

Fragile put out his one good hand for Shane to shake, "Jacob. Dr. Jacob Daedalus actually. But, it's all right. You can call me Fragile. Everybody does."

"Were we friends, Fragile? Uh… I mean you and this Cole guy? Cause I can't help but feel like I can trust you and that we were friends or something," Shane asked, thinking it sounded rather silly and immediately wishing he hadn't said it.

But, Fragile ignored him. "I always thought I had not done enough, if I had found you before you split," Fragile spoke these words softly, almost as much to himself as to Shane. "All of those years ago. But I was so happy to have found you alive. I overlooked the obvious… maybe on purpose. Perhaps I wanted to believe that everything was going to be fine. If only I had found more of you earlier, before all the duplicates got separated. I didn't want to believe I had let her down, and I did, nonetheless," Fragile adjusted in his seat, attempting to give his crippled limbs a chance to stretch after the long day.

He exhaled slowly, blinking sudden tears out of his deep set eyes, before saying, "I am so deeply sorry my old colleague, Van, never got an opportunity to see some of the amazing things that her glorious laboratory mistake could do. Indeed, our calculations of the power and magnitude you would come to possess were terribly underestimated, to say the least." Fragile laughed to himself.

"When we created you everything changed. We didn't figure out the secret to eternal life. We created another weapon of mass destruction that was going to be unleashed upon the world once they figured out how to control you. Van and I planned to get you out of the facility before that could happen. But something went wrong, perhaps Director Gray found out about our plans. Nevertheless, Van had to take you earlier than we had intended. I tried my best to keep you safe."

Shane now knew why he had known Fragile before and not only from Cole's memories either. "Deida?" Shane whispered his recognition. "But what happened to you?" The flood of images and memories that came rushing into his mind looked nothing like the old man sitting beside him.

"I knew they would come for you even in those tunnels they would find you eventually. I had to somehow stop them. I waited until they were sure they had us trapped. But once inside with me it was they who were trapped and I blew the entire building up expecting it would kill everyone, myself included in the process." Fragile said with a sardonic smile, "Instead it left me like this."

"Who's Van?" asked Shane.

Fragile dug inside his coat's breast pocket and handed something to Shane. It was a very old photograph of a much younger Fragile and a smiling Evangeline Murray holding a baby, taken the day the

P.R.I.M.E. was born.

"Van is actually short for Evangeline, she was—" Fragile explained, "Well, I guess you could say that she was your original mother."

The old man let Shane take this information in and ask his own questions when he was ready. When Shane said nothing and sat there staring at the old photograph, Fragile continued on, "Especially if you take into account the fact that on the scientific team that made you, she was the only woman, and Van was the one who cared enough about you to give her own life to save you. Yes, I do believe one could say she was as close to a mother as one possibly gets."

The two of them fell silent after that. Shane was too drained from the day to ask the old guy anymore questions for now. Shane quietly studied the photograph of his 'mother' for several minutes before silently handing the picture back to Fragile without a word. The two of them drove on for a time like that, each of them lost in their own thoughts.

— — — — —

Full Moon. Shane thought quietly to himself, as he gazed out of the passenger side window. Fragile quickly ran through some ground rules, which amounted to going on with life, as if everything were normal, and he would be in contact soon on how to proceed. Shane listened as the old man explained that because they did not recover the envelope along with the money, plans and timelines would need to be adjusted accordingly.

Most of the details Shane barely could keep track of, so he gave up trying and simply repeated, "Sounds good," over and over again, until they reached Shane's home.

The enormous full moon was high in the night's sky, when Fragile pulled up to Shane's home. His heart jumped seeing his mom's car parked in the driveway. Shane felt more exhausted than he had ever been in his entire life. He desperately wished to see his dog and crash onto his bed. Shane felt as if he could sleep for a week.

Shane pulled Cole's knife out from his jacket and handed it to Fragile. "Here, I guess I won't be needing this anymore."

"Where did you get this?" Fragile was shocked to learn that Shane even had the weapon all of this time in the first place.

"It was in Cole's jacket the whole time. I'm glad I never needed to use it. Not that I would have known how to anyway." Shane answered honestly.

"Oh, trust me son. You would have known how to handle it." Fragile said simply as he pocketed the knife and pulled the car to a stop.

"Bye, Fragile, and thanks for all the great memories. I guess we'll be in touch," was Shane's sarcastic goodbye to the old man, as he quickly jumped out of the car and rushed inside without bothering to look back.

"Mom?" Shane called out, as he opened the door to their home. But, before he could turn on the light switch, something made Shane freeze. He could sense someone was in the house. Someone who did not belong.

His blood went cold as ice when he saw Trent and Manny. Two nightmares standing there in the shadowy darkness of his living room.

"Hi there, how you doing, buddy?" Trent asked in a cheery voice, "Shane Fisher, right? You know, you sure look a lot like a guy we know named Cole. But, forget all of that. Has anyone ever told you what a nice little place you've got here?" Shane then saw the flash of a sharp blade suddenly appear in Trent's hand, "Well Shane, I'm only going to ask you this once. Where is our money?"

CHAPTER 12
HOME SWEET HOME

Shane was petrified. The fear was a hurricane inside his head commanding every nerve ending within him not to move. Saying please don't do this. He was taken totally off guard, as he had been in the bank earlier, rendered speechless and unable to react.

"Oh, are you surprised to see us? Well, we took care of Chuppa and his boys, didn't we, Manny? Thanks to all that nice hardware we still had from the bank job. We had enough gear to take on a small army, let alone a couple of stupid bikers."

"Chuppa really thought he had us ambushed, when we went to that public storage unit," Manny said. "I splattered the brains of one of his 'brothers' all over his sorry ass, as they came in after us." Manny loved telling stories, and this was going to be one he told often. "Poor Chuppa, he cried like a woman, once all his biker amigos went bye-bye."

"How did you find me? How did you know where I live?" Shane asked. He was stunned at the nightmare he suddenly found himself in.

Trent answered this, "The computer geek told us all about you, before he took a bullet in the head. Told us how you showed up out of nowhere during the bank job. Really confused the hell out of Jeff who was watching the whole thing going down on the video surveillance cameras. Must have spooked the crap out of Cole too, which was probably why the guy freaked and went so far off plan like he did." Trent chuckled to no one in particular. "Jeff even figured out your name, work, social security number, you name it. He was a good little hacker that kid. I'm really going to miss him," Trent said with mock sadness.

"After that, it was easy tracking you down. Oh, and we found this in with the bags of money," Trent held up a manila envelope, and Shane was certain it was the one Fragile had been so desperate to find, "and I'll bet you know what the crap inside it means. Something like this doesn't just happen to travel alongside all of that money for no reason. Any ideas?" Trent waved the envelope at Shane, as he walked over to the coat closet. Not needing it anymore, Trent set the envelope that he was holding down on the small table next to the closet.

"Nothing? Maybe you need some motivation to jar your memory," Trent said, as he opened the closet door and out tumbled Shane's half-conscious mother. Her arms were bound together at the wrist and she was gagged. She wore a look of sheer terror and confusion, as she searched around the room. Her eyes froze, when they met Shane's. He immediately saw that she was bleeding profusely from the area above her left eye socket. Her broken form fell into the hallway knocking over a small table, spilling umbrellas, hats and various sports equipment, including a pair of Shane's old roller-blades and a baseball bat.

"And look who we found when we got here, your mommy," Trent seized Rebecca by her hair, the pain bringing her to full consciousness, her eyes growing wide in horror.

"Hey, stop! You don't need to do that. Please!" Shane pleaded with the vile little villain.

"Are you stupid or something? I'll do exactly as I like." To prove his point, he gave Rebecca another vicious jerk, causing her to sob through the gag.

Trent was pissed now, "I'm only going to ask you this one more time. Where is the money?"

"I don't know, I didn't get out of…" Shane sputtered, his eyes locked on his mother's, but it was too long for Trent.

"You know what? You're taking too long." Trent shoved Rebecca towards Manny, "Manny, take this old whore to the back room and do with her whatever you want. Have a good time with her, you know what I'm saying, big guy?"

A low growl came from outside in the yard and interrupted Trent. It was Bear looking into the room through the sliding glass door. The normally silent dog pawed at the door hopelessly, as Manny took Rebecca to the back bedroom, slamming the door shut behind them.

"And Manny, after you're done with the mom, please shoot that damn dog," Trent called out over his shoulder with a chuckle, turning back towards Shane, a vicious grin smeared across his face. "Good, now that we aren't distracted, maybe you will start remembering where my money is."

This is it. We are going to die. Shane told himself, desperately trying to fight off the overwhelming feeling of hopelessness. With nothing left to lose, he figured he must at least try to fight them for his mom. Shane took a deep breath and let it out slowly. It would not be his last one, he told himself trying to summon the courage of what he must do next.

"Ok you little bastard. You want to die tonight? Then let's do this!" Shane screamed. Unfortunately, Shane had given the knife he had been carrying around all day in his jacket pocket to Fragile a short time before. So he picked up the nearest weapon within his reach.

The baseball bat. The grip and weight felt right in his hands.

Adrenaline was now coursing through him, and to his own surprise, Shane was ready to fight, preferably someone short who reminded him of vermin. Shane gripped the baseball bat in his hands and readied himself.

Perhaps, it was out of fear for his mother, if he didn't act quickly. Maybe, it was Trent, threatening his dog, or perhaps it was exhaustion, but for whatever reason, for the first time in his life: Shane Fisher was not afraid.

Trent came directly at him, and was all confidence and evil conceit, "I think I am going to cut out small pieces of you. Let you look at them for a while. Identify them. You know? See how well you know human anatomy. I'm going to enjoy seeing how many pieces of you I can remove before you die!" Trent's mouth was running a mile a minute now. Trent liked to torment his victims, before they died. The knife in his hands gave Trent confidence. He slowly advanced towards Shane, "Let's first see how you react to the sight of your own blood?"

Trent moved quickly, feinting left then right administering sharp vicious slashes to Shane's hands and arms. What Shane thought he lacked in fighting skills, he made up for in superior size and intelligence, because he knew he had the reach advantage. With fast swipes of his bat, Shane temporarily kept Trent's deadly knife at a distance.

Ultimately, Shane was no fighter and definitely not a ruthless killer like Trent. Trent changed his strategy suddenly and brought his razor sharp blade down through Shane's shoe, piercing through pinning his foot to the ground. Shane thought he heard the flesh and bone tearing as Trent viciously twisted the blade deeper into the floor.

Shane screamed and fell to the floor instantly. Perhaps, the extreme pain broke control over himself, but for an instant, something automatic took over Shane's reflexes. Without thinking what he was doing, Shane fluidly pulled the knife out of his foot and threw it at Trent with practiced skill. He even managed to hit the vicious little killer in the left arm before Trent kicked Shane in the head, jumping on his back and pinning Shane underneath him. Trent never spoke a word, as he silently removed his own blade from his arm and raised Shane's head in order to quietly slit his throat and put an end to this nuisance for good.

Shane resigned himself to the fact that he was going to die. He tried to be brave, tried to die the way he thought a man should. The way Cole would.

But from out of nowhere, a hand shot out and twisted Trent's right arm, holding the knife behind him so hard that Shane could hear a snapping sound, right before Trent let out a blood-curdling cry.

It was Cole.

But this time, not Cole inside his head messing with Shane's memories and attitude, this was the living breathing person suddenly standing before them. And he was completely naked.

Shane watched in silent amazement, as Cole picked Trent up off the ground with one hand and put the knife directly between his eyes with the other hand.

Trent was dead instantly. The end of a wicked little butcher who had hurt so many.

Shane's replicant, Cole, instantly absorbed back into Shane, before Trent's corpse even hit the floor. The killer's dead weight landed on top of him.

It all happened so fast, like Cole had never been there at all. Shane experienced a small wave roll through his body and mind, like in the bank. But this time, instead of the strong and sharp jolt of light rocking his entire body, it felt more like a shiver. His mind again was filled with the gruesome images of what had happened only this time from Cole's viewpoint of plunging the knife into Trent's skull. Distracted by this, he did not yet have time to consider the fact that he had controlled his duplicating abilities. Making them into a weapon.

Along with these new memories, Shane felt a warm tingling sensation in his foot, where up until a moment before, he had been writhing, almost black-ing-out in pain from Trent's vicious knife attack. Shane stared down in awed disbelief at his bloodied shoe, but felt the injury was gone.

Healed?… Regenerated was more like it. Shane thought, as he stared down at his now uninjured foot. Somehow, when he re-absorbed the unhurt Cole back into himself, the stab injury that Trent had inflicted upon his foot had miraculously disappeared, leaving, except for the blood, no trace that a wound was ever there to begin with. Shane's hand went up reflexively to touch his head where he had been hurt earlier that day in the bank. Nothing. Both his hand and head wounds from earlier had also been healed by creating and then re-absorbing Cole. Shane had no idea how something like this was even possible outside the realm of movies and comic books, let alone the fact that he had never been able to do anything like this before in his life.

He was beginning to understand at least this much; Cole was him and he was Cole, which meant, Shane was beginning to realize, he potentially could do what Cole could do. (If he figured out how to) and if need be, he could actually produce or manifest another physical form of himself.

How is that even possible? Shane wasn't sure if all of this was a hallucination, and he was in some insane asylum drooling on himself.

Shane had little time to reflect on this or on the killer's passing, because a deep distorted sort of howl-ing scream rang out from behind him. Shane turned in time to see Manny barreling down on him at a dead run. The giant's berserk rage sent Shane clear across the room with a single blow.

Manny merely glanced at his friend Trent's corpse, as he again charged towards where Shane's dazed body had just landed. Manny was totally engulfed in his own fury and fantasized twisted evil thoughts of torture while he began relentlessly kicking Shane.

The first of Manny's stomping blows landed on Shane's spine. Manny's boot struck the spot a few inches below the neck, between the shoulder blades sending a cold electric shockwave down Shane's legs. Having lost count of the vicious blows after four, Shane thought he could make out a voice shouting at him but yet somehow the sound seemed distant and far away. As if its source came down a long hallway rather than from directly above him.

"Do you hear me!?" It was Manny screaming, "I'm gonna set your open mouth against the street curb outside and kick the back of your head in with my boot. I think I might even force your stupid mommy to watch me do it." Apparently Manny enjoyed the taunting game every bit as much as Trent did after all.

From out of nowhere, Rebecca jumped onto Manny's back. With her arms still bound in front of her, she had followed the big man down the hallway and was trying to strangle him from behind. Her shirt was ripped open and she was naked from the waist down, but she wrapped her bare legs around the giant, determined to stop him from killing her son.

Tears were streaking down her swollen face, soaking the gag that was still secure in her mouth, while she futilely struggled to slow the beast down. But Manny threw her off of him hard towards the floor effortlessly with one arm, never taking his murderous gaze off of Shane. Manny's twisted mind was already imagining how he would beat and torture Shane until almost senseless, rape his mother in front of him before finally killing them both. In his mind that was the way he should mourn the death of his only friend, Trent. Through revenge and cruelty.

Manny picked Shane's seemingly lifeless body up too easily, preparing to follow through with his threat. He gripped Shane in both arms and began squeezing and crushing him with incredible strength.

Unfortunately for Manny, Cole knew how to kill. In addition, his father's training in southern praying mantis Kung Fu, the most deadly and secret martial art form in the world, meant Shane was now trained in it as well. Lying possum prone Shane had prepared his body to take in as much air as possible, inflating his chest cavity massively as he was lifted off the ground like a doll. Before Manny could react to what was happening, Shane rapidly let out the air in his lungs giving himself enough room to move his arms within the giant ox's deadly grasp. In the same fluid motion Shane released himself from Manny's grip and released a flurry of lightning speed Jet Choi/Ping Choi/Phoenix punches into the big man's ribs, collarbone and throat, crushing the bones with each hit. Before pushing his fingers deep into Manny's eye sockets, completely and permanently destroying them by removal from his giant skull.

How did I do that? The reflexive actions he had performed astonished Shane as he dropped the eyeballs to the floor and stepped on them.

But, things were not over yet. Now blinded, Manny thrashed around like a bull in a china shop. Smashing and screaming into everything around him. Shane pulled his mother out of the way, before the gargantuan's mass came down upon her. Shane quickly picked up the baseball bat and with two precise blows stopped Manny's wild thrashing. Permanently.

"Are you ok?" Shane asked his mom removing the gag from around her mouth and freeing her arms.

"I…I'm not sure–I don't think I can answer that. Everything that happened, Shane…I don't understand what's going on…" was all she could say, before closing her eyes and slumping to the floor, quietly sobbing.

Shane noticed an eerie silence settling over the house. *Maybe I'm in shock*, he thought, as he checked to make certain the rest of the house was secure. Like when the music of a film's score drops to silence for dramatic effect, somewhere in the background of his mind, he could see his mother still crying on the floor, Bear still barking outside the sliding glass door. Yet, Shane could hear none of it. He looked around at the chaos that was all around him and simply felt numb.

He walked over with a new set of clothes for his mother, crouched down next to her huddled form on the ground and placed a blanket around her. It didn't appear that she had been badly hurt, but she was definitely going to need some time. Utterly spent, Shane could only collapse down next to her on the floor. The two, mother and son sat like that for a while, silently surveying the total chaos that was their house for the first time.

"What the hell just happened!?–" Rebecca's voice cracked, as she asked the question.

Shane didn't exactly understand any of this himself, and he sat there staring at the floor in silence.

After a time, Shane attempted to speak in order to reassure his mother that everything was going to be alright, but the words wouldn't come. How could he explain to her the crazy things that had happened to him without her thinking he was an absolute lunatic?

"So…this is all somehow tied up with the bank thing I heard about on the news earlier?" Rebecca questioned, still unsure of what was really going on. "But, why did they come here? Why follow you and how did they even know–" She referred to the two corpses that were now lying on the floor in the middle of the living room.

Shane cut her off by standing up. He needed to show her something but wasn't even sure how to even try it. He stood there for a while with his eyes closed concentrating, but felt foolish almost instantly. He was about to give up the attempt, when he heard his mom give out a loud audible gasp, calling out his name, "Shane!?"

Shane opened his eyes to once again find Cole standing there alongside him. Completely nude and smiling his usual sardonic grin.

Now, it was Rebecca's turn to think she had gone mad. She was seeing double or something, because after Shane had stood up, where there had been only one, now stood two of her sons.

"Hi there," the duplicate said to her shamelessly from behind Shane, still smiling.

"Cole?" Shane asked, still unbelieving of his new-found ability.

"The one and only, but please, Cole was only the name I used for the last several years. Please allow me to introduce myself formally. Apparently, my real name is Shane Fisher, and it is a pleasure to meet you." He held his hand out in mock greeting.

Rebecca looked from one Shane to the other and could not believe the information her eyes were telling her. "Shane, please tell me what the hell is going on? And why is there a naked you standing in our living room?" she asked, not entirely sure if the trauma from everything that had happened might have caused her to snap. His mom looked as though she might begin to hyperventilate.

Not wanting to overly frighten and confuse his mother, Shane quickly re-absorbed his duplicate, before turning to her to calm her down, "Take it easy, mom. I know all of this is really strange. Look, I'm still trying to figure it all out myself. But…" He trailed off, not quite sure what to say. "Well, I guess I better start from the beginning."

The words came out slowly at first, and after a time, he told his mother everything that had happened. The entire confusing day, beginning with being caught in the middle of a bank robbery, to the first time he absorbed his 'Cole' replicant along with all of the memories that came with it. Waking up afterwards, thinking he was going crazy having someone else's memories fighting for dominance inside of him and threatening to tear apart his identity. He recounted the mission he took with Fragile to recover the stolen money, the van. He described finding Jeff's corpse, hiring Chuppa and thinking he was out of danger. He told her about Wayne, everything he could think of. As he was speaking, he realized how strange and fantastical the events were, beyond the realm of possibility. Everything, except for the ability to duplicate and re-absorb replicants of himself. Even after hearing Fragile's explanation of the process, he wasn't quite sure how it worked exactly. He had no rational explanation for it and saying it out loud didn't make any more sense out of it. In fact, it made all of it sound more bizarre. Like he was reading one of the science fiction novels from his store.

When he was done, he was sure his mother would tell him that he was crazy or that he was a liar, but considering all she had seen and been through that day, how could she?

"So, let me get this straight… you're saying you now have this other man's memories from the last decade or so? Including being raised by other parents? How is that even possible? This isn't making any sense. I–" She asked. She was struggling to hold her confusion and emotions in check. "Let alone the ability to create this physical incarnate, Cole?"

"I'm not quite sure," Shane answered truthfully, "but regardless of figuring out what is going on with me, what are we going to do with all this?" He waved his hand at the destruction that used to be their quaint living room. "Should we call the cops? What the hell would we tell them? They would lock me up in a loony bin or jail. Not to mention that guy Wayne would come kill me, if this all came to light. Maybe…" Shane trailed off, an idea coming to mind. He ran to his bedroom to fetch an additional pair of clothes and made Cole reappear again. Shane waited for Cole to get dressed and return to the living room before he spoke to his duplicate.

"C-C-Cole–" Shane fumbled for words, "uh-, I mean Shane or whoever, look, can you handle this?–" Shane asked his duplicate, "My mom and I, I mean we both–" Shane motioned to his mother, "aren't exactly experts at the whole disposing of diabolical mass-murderers and stuff like that. Neither of us can really afford to take time off or, you know, go to jail and stuff. I mean we're kinda living hand-to-mouth right now. Any chance you can help us make this, well, you know… uh, kinda go away?"

The corpses of Trent and Manny were still very much in the living room. And both Shane and his mother wanted them out. Now.

"What do you think this is exactly? This isn't some movie," Cole said, looking extremely stressed all of a sudden, "I can't simply make a call and have someone over here wearing a tuxedo to clean this place up."

Then after a brief pause for dramatic effect, Cole burst into laughter, as he leaned over and pulled his phone out from Shane's pocket. "I'm joking with you, man. Of course, I know people who can clean this place. But I'm not so sure they'll be wearing tuxedos, I'm afraid."

Cole dialed a number and simply said, "Cole," followed by Shane's address, before hitting the end call button on his phone.

Next, Cole said to them, "Someone will be here very soon, and you both might want to take the dog and drive around the block for a while. Or, why don't you guys go to the emergency room and have that gash above her eye checked out?"

Cole glanced down to examine what was left of Manny after the baseball bat, then up at Shane. A dark smile spread across his face, Cole amended, "Actually, you'd better let me call you when I'm done cleaning this up. Your son here really did a number on this guy."

Rebecca didn't need more of an invitation to get out of there than that. She already felt like she was going into shock and might be sick. She rose to her feet, grabbed Bear and walked out the door into the night; without a word to either of the two men in the room who looked like her son. Cole walked over to Shane before he followed his mother out and conspiratorially whispered, "Oh, and regarding living hand-to-mouth, don't forget that little offshore account I've been keeping. But don't worry, you'll remember all about it soon enough," Cole tapped his head and winked.

Shane looked around one last time at the ruins

that were his home and felt the pangs of exhaustion wash over him like a wave. He wondered what Cole would do as he waited for the cleaners to arrive.

A short time later, seven individuals, five men and two women, arrived at the door. Without a word or acknowledgment that Cole was even there, for that matter, they immediately assessed the situation and began cleaning it up.

Even from the first time Wayne had given him the contact info, Cole always marveled at how absolutely unremarkable any of them were. They were never the same people and all wore common street clothes appropriate for the weather at that time of year, and none of them had any distinguishing characteristics, such as a scar, a tattoo or an unusual physical gesture. Cole felt these people were almost unnatural in how ordinary they were.

When it was all over, Cole couldn't help but respect the practiced efficiency with which these unmemorable men and women silently removed Trent and Manny's corpses and meticulously and emotionlessly disposed of any remaining incriminating evidence.

When they had finished, all seven left exactly the way they had arrived, without a word, leaving Cole alone, waiting for Shane and his mother to return home.

— — — — —

A few hours later, after reabsorbing Cole, Shane noted how completely calm the house was. The house was still a mess, but at least all signs of the two corpses, Trent and Manny, had been completely erased by Cole's cleaners.

Yeah, it was kinda like a movie. Shane laughed darkly to himself at Cole's earlier remark.

His mom came in from her bedroom. She had three small stitches above her eye, but otherwise seemed to be all right.

Like the first time his mind had merged with Cole's in the bank, he saw searing flashes of the other's memories. Again, Shane was haunted by the other man's loss of his wife and family. *Or is it my family now?*

"Mom?" He mumbled, before realizing his mistake.

"Huh? Hold on a second. I can't hear anything with this horse you call a dog wagging." Bear had returned behind his mother, "Did you say something?"

"Are you all right?" Rebecca asked her son, seeing Shane's pale complexion.

"I'm ok. I just don't feel so good and my head is spinning. Maybe I'd better sit down for a minute."

"Let me help you." Rebecca grabbed her son's arm and led him to the couch where she laid him down and placed a small pillow under his head and a light blanket over him.

"I'm fine really, and besides, you are the one who got beat up by those scumbags." Shane said, but was still unable to shake the feeling he had of seeing his murdered wife. *No. That was Cole's wife. Come on, Shane, keep it together.* Shane commanded himself. Fearing he was beginning to lose his own identity. But despite this internal reprimand, Shane's mind wandered back in time. He eventually broke out of this nostalgic memory by something enormous jumping on top of him.

It was his dog, Bear. The playful beast landed on top of the blanket, probably aiming to take dibs on the majority of the pillow that was currently occupied by Shane's head.

What a freaking zoo? Shane thought he almost heard the Cole in him grumble. The absolute mundane nature of this was somehow comforting to him.

"You sure you're all right?" His mom asked, walking towards him from the kitchen with two cups of hot tea. Rebecca sat down next to Shane, holding one of the steaming cups out for her son to take.

"I'm fine, really." Shane reassured her, as he took his tea. "What about you? How are you holding up?"

Tears were already running down his mother's cheeks. "Shane, I– I– just completely lost my mind. I was so worried when those horrible men came into the house…" she wept quietly to herself, but hadn't the energy and soon stopped.

For a while they simply sat there together, mother and son, in silence until his mother rose and went off to her room for sleep. Leaving Shane and the dog alone on the couch.

Exhausted would be an understatement for how Shane felt. He told himself that this day had been some kind of nightmare. A labyrinth of doors he had needed to cross before reaching this place, it felt almost surreal to him, watching his dog Bear dozing off next to him. He had somehow made it out alive and safe.

Earlier, those two considerations were an unimaginable luxury. Even Bear, was contently snoring in his usual spot next to him on the couch.

Eventually, after carrying himself to bed, Shane drifted into a deep sleep under the silver-blue light of the full moon shining in through the window.

— — — — —

Hours later, after dawn, Shane awoke in a cold sweat from night terrors that had been raging in his mind. Visions and images that were completely foreign and yet somehow familiar. He tried to calm and persuade himself back to sleep, but soon, he gave up. He had to know more. His mind was racing with questions.

He got out of bed quietly, careful not to disturb his mother in the next room, and went to the kitchen, unconsciously opening the refrigerator and staring in at its contents before aimlessly closing it again. He wasn't even hungry and chuckled at the fact that so many people perform this same banal ritualistic habit.

He went into the living room, sunk into the couch and considered watching some television, but soon dismissed the idea. He didn't wish to zone out and forget. He wanted to remember. Shane needed answers.

He put the spare set of clothes on the couch and paced the room trying to summon Cole, but nothing happened. After a few minutes of trying, Shane gave up and sat down on the couch again, frustrated. He thought earlier that he understood how to conjure his duplicate, but somehow it wasn't working now. He tried to relax and closed his eyes.

"I notice you're getting the hang of that trick of yours," he heard his own voice say.

Shane's eyes snapped open and saw Cole was there, suddenly seated next to him, relaxing on the couch, as if this were perfectly normal.

Cole could tell Shane was not understanding him. "Absorbing the memories and abilities of the duplicates, that I could do, but actually re-releasing them again. Never." Cole explained.

Cole examined Shane up and down as if seeing him for the very first time before saying, "So the actual P.R.I.M.E., the original source of it all has at last been found," Cole said as much to himself as to Shane. "You know, I really could have used that ability when I was on active duty. Oh yeah, and now that I am back being a part of you, I have to request you get this insomnia thing under control," Cole said sarcastically, before yawning.

Shane ignored his confident alter-ego, "What do you mean, you're Shane Fisher?" Shane was now even more confused than he had thought he was. "I'm Shane Fisher. And, I am not some bank robbing murderer who—"

"Yes, you are," Cole cut him off, "You are me, but I think even more accurate would be to say that I am you. You see, Shane, I am your replicant, your exact duplicate. After you absorbed me, my memories became your memories. My abilities and all that I have learned, since you made me, are now yours. This includes all of my joy and pain, my hopes and dreams, my failures and successes. For better or worse, like it or not, they're all yours now. If you relaxed and allowed it, you'd find you would be able to remember everything about me, or rather you. Including for that matter all of the duplicates that I have been able to absorb over the last year or so. And trust me there are a lot of them." Cole could see the color drain from Shane's face, "Hey cheer up. It's not all bad… for instance did you know I, Ur–I mean, you can speak over four languages so far. Fluently. That's pretty cool, huh? And trust me, that's only the beginning of it."

Cole's attempts at humor weren't working at that particular moment. Shane was feeling worse. "But, how did I not know you existed? How come I didn't know I had this power? And, where did it come from?" Shane had more questions, but figured he'd better start with those.

"That I do not know. When I saw you on the video monitor back in the van, I figured you were another duplicate for me to absorb. But, a part of me always knew the day would come when I would run into a duplicate that was more Alpha than me. After all, I don't have any of my own memories that reach further back than when you initially made me. A long time ago. None of the duplicates do. That's when you first made us. All of those memories are actually yours. It's actually funny to think, I never really considered it until I met Fragile and absorbed my first duplicate. I guess I always figured kids don't really remember the details of their childhood that much before a certain age. You know like still frame images and impressions or something." Cole answered honestly.

"I made you? How did I do that?" Shane was getting frustrated now. If he was the creator, then how come he had no memories or even the knowledge that he even possessed such abilities, let alone why he had them?

"I don't know those answers. All I know is that I was created by you to acquire experiences and abilities and to live a unique and separate life from yours, perhaps indefinitely, which I have. Perhaps it might have to do with what your goal or intention is at the time you make us. Or maybe you made us when you were too young, not fully developed yet or something. Who knows? But I do know that after you re-absorbed me, I knew all about you and your life Shane Fisher, because I am you now." Cole reported his best current theory, but not without a touch of sadness. Then, he added, "Perhaps, one of the others might have the answers to your questions?"

"There are more duplicates out there like you, uh, like me… more of my replicas?" Shane asked, starting to feel sick and dizzy. A part of him already knew the answer.

"Yeah, there are a more of them," Cole answered casually with his usual confidence. "Are you ready to join the hunt? Because you're in it, whether you like it or not, and you're gonna find out real quickly that not all duplicates necessarily want to meet their P.R.I.M.E." Suddenly, the smile was gone from Cole's face. He was a mere replicant, a shadow to Shane's

P.R.I.M.E. nature, his skills and training will help aid in their mutual survival. But, that mostly depended on Shane, and the speed in which he could learn to integrate and control his new powers and accept the mind-synthesis that occurred with each new duplicate he absorbed. "Some will even try to kill you, rather than chance being tested by an initial contact or touch and re-absorbed by you. Trust me, I know." Cole warned the new P.R.I.M.E..

Shane had nervously begun to clean and pick up various items that had fallen out of the coat closet where Trent and Manny had kept his mother. "I am pretty sure I don't understand anything that you're saying," Shane sputtered, "Join what hunt? And why am I the P.R.I.M.E.? Clearly you can see that there is nothing dominant or Alpha about me. The only reason I don't think I have gone totally insane and having a conversation with myself right now is on account that my mom saw you too." Shane sighed deeply, "Maybe it's like Fragile said. Maybe I need more time to process all of this." Shane had replaced everything to its proper place in the closet and returned the small table right side up again, when he noticed an envelope, the one Trent had set down on the table earlier.

"What's this?" Shane wondered picking it up.

"Let me see that," Cole quickly snatched the envelope out of Shane's hands and tore it open, scanning the contents before saying. "Looks like it is time to wake up the old man," Cole said, picking up his phone. "Fragile, it's Cole. Yes, Cole. Somehow, Shane released me again. But listen this is important. Trent and Manny were here waiting for him, but we took care of them," Cole winked at Shane when he said this. "Best of all, we found the envelope. It's exactly like you said, we have all the information we'll need." Cole listened to Fragile's questions over the phone before answering, " Yeah, all of them. A little over a week from today, nine days. I know that's not much time to prepare, but at least we've got it–"

Shane could not hear what Fragile was saying on the other line, but Cole's face revealed the old man was asking multiple questions that Cole didn't seem to have the answers for.

"I don't have a clue as to how, but Shane has learned how to release and re-absorb his replicants. That's how I'm talking to you now. The synthesis seems to be faster than ever before, and to top it off, he has some kind of new healing ability when he integrates and re-absorbs his duplicates." Cole waited, listening to more of Fragile's questions before continuing, "Yeah, well, I sure could have used that healing trick over the past couple of years. But, why do you think this ability manifested itself now?" Cole asked. "Ok, but we better move quickly. We now know when and where but not how long they're all going to be there. This might be our last shot at finding them. Shane will leave the envelope at the usual drop location for you to pick up in the morning." before pressing a button on the phone, ending the call.

"Shane, you need to, once and for all, really come to terms with this fact moving forward." Cole looked Shane in the eyes when he said this, "I am you. But,

I am a part of you. A very small part." Cole's smile, if only slightly, was back again, "For a while, a long time ago, I thought I was the P.R.I.M.E. With all the duplicates I've absorbed over the years and given our age, one would have thought I was at least pretty close, right? But then again I could never do what you could do." Cole laughed out loud at this. But, his mood grew more serious, when he said, "Shane Fisher, I've come to know that whether you are or are not the P.R.I.M.E. doesn't really matter. What matters is that there are more of you out there, and they will be coming for you." Cole handed Shane the envelope, what Cole and Fragile had been searching for all along.

Shane examined the contents of the envelope. It was packed with fourteen dossiers filled with information on individuals, but only one of them meant anything to him. Only one frightened him. The one with his name on it.

'SHANE FISHER - P.R.I.M.E.', was written across the top of the dossier. The packet contained photographs and information on every imaginable aspect of his life: where he lived, worked, phone records, credit card statements, names of friends and acquaintances and even information on his mother, Rebecca. His entire life neatly presented and contained in a single file folder.

Cole answered before Shane could even formulate the question, "What it means is you are very lucky we found you when we did. If we hadn't intercepted this, and it had reached the hands of Director Gray--" But Cole didn't elaborate. "I wonder though, was it just blind luck that brought us together? Perhaps there was another cause to our meeting, other unseen forces at work?"

"Like what?" Shane asked.

"Like you." Cole answered, "Every duplicate I have ever absorbed has always found me. It was as if they were drawn to me. So, maybe I was pulled towards you, with or without the envelope being our focus?"

Shane didn't know how to respond to this news. Instead he studied the other contents of the envelope. In addition to the fourteen dossiers there was also a black and white photograph of a luxurious hotel with a single date and time hand written in red capital letters across the bottom. The date was nine days away. Shane identified in the photo's background the Temple Mount and its Western Wall, in Israel, from a trip he and his mother had taken years ago. The hotel was located somewhere in The Old City of Jerusalem.

What Shane didn't yet know is that he was looking at the next time and meeting place of all thirteen Directors of the Cabal.

Cole could tell this was too much information for Shane. He needed time to process the duplicate fusion, let alone come up with a game plan of how to proceed. "You need to get that envelope to Fragile right away. He'll help you figure out what to do next. The old man's your best chance at surviving what is coming next."

When Shane didn't respond to this advice Cole said, "Better pack your bags. I guess you're headed to

Israel. And by the way–get my knife back from Fragile. Trust me you're gonna need it." Cole said, before
putting his hand on Shane's shoulder and disappearing
again.

CHAPTER 13
A RETURN TO SANITY?

"Hey, sleepy head, wake up. It's Saturday morning. Don't you have a manager meeting today?" his mother asked, shaking Shane gently.

"Huh, what? Did I really fall asleep here? Like this?" Shane quietly asked. He had fallen back asleep on the couch and apparently, Bear had come and joined him as well. The ninety-pound pooch had Shane pinned under his snoring bulk. It appeared the dog had even less intention than Shane of getting up at that particular moment. Shane attempted to shift away from the light and roll over, but the furry animal on top of him made it virtually impossible.

Was yesterday all a bad dream? Shane hoped. He was enjoying the sheer mundane routine-like feeling of the morning. Reality, however, settled upon him quickly. His mind clearing of its morning fog was suddenly barraged with not only Cole's life, but dozens of other duplicates that Cole had collected over the years. He tried hopelessly to block them out.

But how do you block out your own memories? And *who the hell is Jackson? Or Clarke?* But Shane already knew that he would be able to answer to either one of those names along with many other identities now.

The night's sleep and rest had made major changes to Shane's brain chemistry and physical composition. The ever so subtle mass increase caused the worst muscle soreness of his life along with what felt to Shane like a migraine headache. So overwhelmed by this, he could merely let out a weak groan.

"Well, I can certainly understand you wanting to call in sick today, but don't forget you left your car in the bookstore parking lot, and Willie said he was going to work on the transmission for you later today after your shift." Rebecca spoke quickly.

Shane knew his mother well enough to know that she did this when she was nervous. Growing up, she often spoke this way when she was on uncertain ground. Like the time she first told him that he was adopted. That was eight years ago and she had been so nervous, and spoke so fast that she accidentally said it twice.

When he had responded to the news by saying, "You're my mommy no matter whose belly I came out of." Shane knew he had relieved her of all her visible worries.

However, on this particular morning he didn't know what or how to alleviate what had happened the day prior or its ramifications going forward. And so he said nothing at all, and she kept speaking in rapid-fire.

"The world keeps turning despite what happens to us. So, you might as well do your shift and make some money, if you're going there anyway, right? Besides, it will be good for you to go back there and settle into your normal routine, don't you think? Here, this will help things get started."

His mother's tone was way too exuberant and happy this morning for Shane. She had cleaned up the rest of the house, had already made coffee, and was handing him a cup, by the time he had managed to shove the enormous dog off of himself and sit up on the couch.

The events of the day before felt like a surreal dream. Shane would have convinced himself it was all a dream too, if not for the fact that he had to concentrate so hard on memories of his own past. This helped to keep Cole's and now the other duplicate's lives from swirling inside his head and taking over too much.

That and his mother had a cut over her black eye.

I won't make it through another day of this. Shane was sure he was going to go mad, living with multiple sets of memories now. *Relax, Shane. Fragile said he thinks it usually took a week or so to acclimate to this mess.* Shane reminded himself.

"I'll drive you to work, but you need to get ready. So, throw that caffeine down, and let's get to it," said his mother, still tiding up the house as she moved. She called to the dog, as she went off to get her keys, "Hey Bear, you want to go for a car ride?" The dog's tail wagged furiously, all signs of sleepiness instantly gone at the notion of going for a ride.

"I've got a better idea," Shane said, as he lifted the cup to his lips and sipped the fresh steaming brew. "Maybe I should take the day off and try to figure out what happened yesterday?"

"But Shane, we can't afford for you to get fired or anything—"

He cut her off quickly. "One, no one is getting fired. Don't forget I have a replacement," Shane said with a grin and snapped his fingers with a flourish as a duplicate, Cole, was suddenly sitting next to him, identical, except for the fact that Cole was wearing a slightly larger smile and covering up his nudity with his hands. "And two," Shane continued, "You and I really need to talk about all of this…" Shane said, waving his hands at Cole for emphasis. "I mean, what am I, for god's sake!? I know you told me that I was adopted before Dad died, but you never mentioned that I am some sort of freakish government experiment or something? I mean normal people can't do this, Mom!" Shane screamed.

He was overcome now. Shane was trying to keep his cool this early in the morning, but was finding it difficult the more he considered the past day's events and revelations. Now add to that all of the other duplicates that Cole had collected over the years. His brain was a reckless ocean of neurons flooding and reconfiguring his mind for him. Even with Cole seated next to him, Shane still retained the other replicants that Cole had brought into him. As if once the initial reabsorption at the bank had occurred, it started an irreversible downloading process of other identities.

"Mom, I am losing myself. Soon I won't know the difference between me and them." Shane choked out his fears to his mother.

Despite her attempts at a sunny disposition on the outside, Rebecca too was feeling more than her fair share of panic and fear for her son. There were a few times last night and this morning that she wanted to grab him and Bear, jump into her car and drive out of there as fast as she could. She didn't care where, so long as it was as far away as possible. But she wouldn't abandon the life she had with her son. Especially, when it seemed he needed her and the stability she had always provided for him now more than ever. Which was precisely why she had woken up and put on a brave and cheery front for him.

So, Rebecca wrapped her arms around her only son, as she always did when Shane was inconsolable. She held him like that for a while, until she could hear his breathing becoming more steady.

Rebecca saw Cole, her son's smiling duplicate on the couch disappear from the corner of her eye, as Shane's posture and bearing suddenly straightened in her arms. She would have sworn his size and mass had increased almost imperceptibly.

She whispered to him, "Ok, Shane. I understand, but I don't think it's such a good idea sending anyone to work your shift except you. Especially not until we figure out what is happening to you."

If you only knew the half of it. Shane thought, but he kept it to himself. After last night's disclosure of the envelope he knew that he, Shane Fisher, was definitely caught up in all of this P.R.I.M.E. business, whatever the hell that may mean. He also knew that being this P.R.I.M.E. allowed him to do some pretty wild things. A reckless, curious part of him wanted nothing more than to explore these new abilities further. However, his mother insisted that he follow through with work himself.

At least I'll be able to pick up a travel book on Israel. Shane thought sarcastically, as he resigned himself to the fact that he was going to Brent & Nigel's.

Of course, she was right, but Shane, even considering how petrified he was of them, couldn't help but entertain the possibility of using these new-found abilities.

If my powers are going to get me killed, I might as well make my mom's and my life better in the meantime, right? He was trying to convince himself of this fact, even as he was putting on his clothes and preparing to go back to his mundane, albeit, safe job.

I am the sum of all my experiences. I guess some habits are hard to break. With the personal identity crisis he was undergoing, Shane couldn't help but laugh at this thought.

— — — — —

Shane's mother dropped him off at the bookstore a little early, and he waited in his car, until a group of employees crowded, waiting for a manager to let them in the side doors. He was extremely anxious regarding how he was going to explain yesterday's sudden disappearance. His fears were immediately alleviated upon seeing Pete with a coffee in each hand waiting for him like usual. The familiar sight comforted Shane, and he smiled at the older man, as he approached the side door.

"Hey, Shane. How's it going, boss man?"

That's odd, I would have thought out of everyone here that Pete would at least ask me why I disappeared yesterday.

"Oh, you know, same as always, Pete. Bruised

from surviving attacks from psychopath bank robbers and fighting off a possible mental dissociative-disorder, like multiple or split-personality paranoia, but still bitter as ever and ready to help people get their read on." Shane laughed, maybe a little too much at the private joke.

Pete noticed something different in Shane for the first time, then said, "Uh, maybe you don't need that first coffee today," joked Pete, taking a sip from the left hand then the right, and then he said, "You look... different somehow, more confident or something."

"Oh, you know, Pete, I've been doing pushups." Shane spoofed back. However, he stopped smiling, when he saw the look on old Peter's face.

Do I really look different? Changed? Can Pete tell there is something wrong with me? Shane wondered, as he opened the door, walked over and disengaged the alarm before returning to the information desk at the center of the store to clock in for the day.

Yeah, I do kinda feel more confident today. Shane smiled to himself.

"Hey, are we having this manager meeting, or are you going to stand there with that stupid grin on your face all day?" It was that arrogant music department manager, Brian.

"Shut up, Brian. Shane's the boss. He'll call the meeting when he damn well pleases." Pete said. The older man was still holding his two cups of coffee, as he spoke, "Hey, Shane, what's on the agenda today? You said you wanted me to attend today's meeting, but do you want me to do the morning deposits and count registers first? Join you guys later?"

Shane had always liked Pete. It was something about his calm demeanor. Today, however, Pete reminded Shane a lot of an air force sergeant, a father he had once had. Cole's father.

I am never going to get used to this! Shane thought to himself, Cole's memories and experiences were still permeating his psyche. Bonding to his own mind and identity. According to Cole last night, Shane was going to need those skills and training in order to survive.

"I think that's a fine idea." Shane replied automatically. "Get things ready for the store to open and join us when you're ready."

"Yes, sir," Pete answered and headed towards the back office to do his morning opening procedures. It was true. Pete couldn't help but notice that Shane held himself a bit differently today.

For some reason, *the kid looks more like a leader today. That's good.* Pete thought to himself.

Shane was watching him go, when all of a sudden, he felt a hand roll across his back and heard a woman's voice from behind, "Are you going to clock in, or are you working for free today?" Angie moved in close to Shane, her body language revealing more than a common liking to her boss.

Shane decided to play it off and ignore the flirtatious gesture, "Yeah, clocking in, not that the pay is much better than working for free anyway. Oh, and I'll take care of that situation with you and Brian in today's meeting." Before leaving the Information Desk and heading for the back to start the manager meeting as he passed the café, he called out, "Hey, Skylar, can you round up the crew for me, so we can begin the meeting. I just need to get something in the back office, and I'll be right out."

"Sure, no problem," Skylar answered, as she placed a batch of muffins in the small oven to bake, while they were meeting. "Also, Shaney, coffee is coming your way in a minute," she added a flirtatious glance his way for good measure.

"Thanks, Sky. As always, you are a godsend," he replied.

It's awful strange how nobody's mentioned my disappearance yesterday. Did anybody even notice I never came back from lunch? Shane thought, before getting on with the day and his morning routine.

— — — — —

"Look," Brian interrupted Shane for the third time in the meeting, "Angie was hired as a 'music department' salesperson. She isn't even trained for the book floor. I mean did you even see her trying to help people find books yesterday? Oh, yeah, I forgot, Fisher, you didn't, because you were too busy trying to play hero to her. As if a girl like Angie would ever go for a nerd turd like you anyhow." Brian got defensive, when the topic of Angie came up at the end of the meeting.

"That's out of line and personal Brian," Skylar said, appalled at his rude behavior. She still couldn't believe she had found Brian attractive when she first started working at Brent & Nigel's a couple of years ago.

It took every ounce of willpower for Shane not to twist the jerk into a pretzel–and for some reason, he knew he now could with Cole's Kung Fu training–but instead Shane calmly replied, "I'm the manager of this place, right? That means you do as I say, and if you want to keep your job, you will shut your mouth and speak only when I ask you a question. When I want your opinion, I'll give it to you. Do you understand me, Brian, or are we going to have a serious problem?" There was such certainty in the way Shane said these last words that the message sent was clear. The last thing Brian had to worry about was losing his job, if he interrupted or spoke out of turn again. Almost everyone in the room felt something different with Shane today. He was acting more like a boss than your friend.

"Shane, I can take her in the cafe. I was going to need to hire someone anyway, and she worked out great for me yesterday when I needed her," Skylar broke the silence.

"Perfect. Brian, please take Angie off the music department schedule. Skylar, you've got her in the cafe from this point forward," Shane said with final authority letting the group know the subject was settled.

Brian slumped down slightly and didn't say a word for the rest of the meeting. Shane called the meeting to an end soon after that.

Shane concluded with, "Thanks, everyone, good meeting, and let's go sell some books!" which resulted in everybody awkwardly staring at him like he was some kind of book nerd cheerleader. Even Pete smiled at this last comment. This sounded more like something the old Shane would say. Overall, Shane thought the day had gone pretty smoothly, considering yesterday's chaos.

And still, no mention about my disappearance.

Shane now focused his attention on finding out what was going on at the bank. He wanted to find out if the cops had any leads or suspects. After all, if they were looking for Cole as a suspect, it was only a matter of time before they found someone who happened to look identical to him working a few stores down. Shane didn't want to be thrown in jail for a crime he didn't commit.

Good old Ray, his friend and manager of the bank next door, could sure talk alot once he got going. "Dude, you wouldn't believe the kind of stuff they have in this place. It is like watching an episode from one of those crime scene investigation shows or something. So freaking cool!" Ray was going nuts over the phone. "But you should already know all this, I mean you gave a statement to the cops yesterday too."

But, that was impossible. I wasn't even here yesterday afternoon. I was busy trying to stay alive surrounded by bank robbers, murderers, thugs and body-doubles. "What are you talking about? I never--," but the realization of what probably happened stopped him from revealing the truth, "Uh, well, I guess I'll see you for lunch then, but Ray--this time you meet me over here." Shane tried to recover a little composure, before he hung up the phone.

After hearing from Ray how they were conducting the investigation, but still had no suspects, Shane was satisfied that the authorities were hunting down a cold trail.

At least I'm not being hunted by the cops. Now, I only have to worry about evil-twins coming and killing me in order to avoid being absorbed by me. Plus, last night, Cole said I had to start hunting them down myself.

Shane was running through different scenarios like this, when Skylar came rushing into the back office.

"Shane, I need you right away. Brian, that ass, is back in my cafe and harassing Angelica. He's telling her that she is not going to have a job much longer, if she doesn't get back into the music department."

"Can't anyone around here deal with that jerk?" Shane asked, tired of the meathead's arrogance. The sexist music manager was really getting on Shane's nerves. Shane was under a lot of stress and interrupting him right now was a really bad idea on Brian's part.

"Actually, we have always been kinda waiting for you to do something about it. You never really have," Skylar said, revealing a truth many of the booksellers had been rumoring for months.

"Well, I'm feeling like a different person today," Shane said getting to his feet. "I think I'll have a talk with Brian and get things settled with him once and for all."

In the past, whenever Skylar had needed Shane to take care of something when it involved Brian, she had always in the back of her mind been nervous, even a little scared for Shane.

This time, however, it was Brian that Skylar worried for.

———

When Shane arrived at the café, he found Brian still cornering Angie in the back. Shane marched over to Brian and, without a word, grabbed him by the shoulders, spinning him until they met eye to eye.

"What the hell do you think you're doing, Fisher?" Brian looked as surprised as he was angry. "Do you really want to go there with me? I've been waiting a long time to have a good reason to put my fist through your face." Brian's confident smile was from ear to ear when he said this.

"Actually, Brian," Shane moved even closer to the bigger guy, "I'm the one who has been waiting a long time for this."

That was enough of a challenge for Brian and, without warning, he threw a punch directly at the bridge of Shane's nose.

Caught by surprise, Shane reacted and lowered his head down a couple of inches, just as Brian's right fist made contact. But, instead of Brian's hand making contact with Shane's soft nose and face, it came down on the hardest part of Shane's skull, above the brow line. A loud snap, crackle, pop sound could be heard across the café, as the bones in Brian's hand broke and fractured.

"Aaah!" Brian squealed in agony. "Christ…I

think you broke my hand. I am going to sue your ass!" Brian screamed at Shane.

"Oh no you're not, Brian," Skylar spoke up now. "We all saw you throw a punch at Shane. It's not his fault you broke your own hand. If anything, it should be Shane going after you with an attorney."

"Nobody is suing anyone," said Shane, as he reached under the counter and took a plastic bag out and filled it with ice. "Brian is going to be taking the rest of the day off to get his hand checked out. And Brian, when you come back to work, make sure your attitude is fixed along with that hand of yours. Here, you'll need this." Shane said, placing the ice into Brian's left hand, the only one that now worked, before spinning the crippled bully around once again and pushing him out of the cafe.

"We're not done, Fisher. Not by a long shot," Brian threatened Shane, as he walked away.

"Yeah, well, anytime you want that other hand broken, you let me know and I will be happy to help you out with that," Shane replied before giving Brian a subtle push towards the café exit.

Shane was walking away from the café, feeling rather good about himself, when he heard a voice from behind call his name.

"Shane, can you wait up a sec?" Angelica called.

"Hey, Angie, sure. What's up? Are you alright?" Shane asked.

"I'm ok. I guess. I want to–" Angie hesitated, "I mean Shane… can we talk? When you get a chance later, of course."

"Sure, Angie, let me get this ship up and running, and we can chat," Shane responded. He could tell something was on Angie's mind, but it would have to wait until the store was open. He could tell whatever was troubling her was not good news at all.

This was only confirmed a couple of hours later, when he found Angie, sitting alone in the break room crying. He asked the other booksellers, but nobody knew what was wrong with her today. Skylar said she remembered Angie practically floating on a cloud of happiness when they were leaving work yesterday.

So, what is bothering Angie like this? She seems fine, except when I come around. I hope she's not upset with me about some-thing? I really don't need another pointless headache to deal with. Shane worried.

Shane's answer came soon enough, when Angie knocked on the door to his back office, stuck her head in the doorway, and asked, "Can I come in? Do you have time for us to talk now?"

Shane shrugged and said, "Of course, Angie, come in, come in."

As he stood up to greet her, Shane noticed that she closed the door behind her. Odd. But, before Shane could think anymore on that, Angie crossed the distance of the room, had both arms around him and was kissing his neck.

"Angie, what the hell are you doing? What's gotten into you? You know this is against store policy.

What is the matter with you!?" Shane pulled himself away from her affections. *Damn, she is amazingly beautiful. And she smells incredible. What is that gardenia? Shut up, Shane. Don't even think it.*

Angie was saying, "Oh, Shane, please. I am so sorry. Whatever I did to make you ignore me today, and you never called me last night, like you said you were going to. I can't take it. I have no idea what I did, but if it's work-related, I will make it up, or I'll quit or whatever. I wanted… I just want you to be like you were before. You don't regret what you said to me yesterday, do you?" Angie's tearful eyes blinked her question up at Shane, who happened to have absolutely no idea what she was talking about.

What did I say to her yesterday that I would now regret? What happened to this poor girl? Because I have no clue! But, he said instead, "Angie, I really wasn't–uh," Shane fumbled for words, "I really wasn't myself yesterday morning."

"But, you said you really always wanted me, and that you'd quit your job today to be with me. You said that you loved the way I was always smiling and always happy, even here at work. And then, you kissed me. Oh my god, what a kiss!" Angie closed her eyes as if to relive the moment. Her eyes opened slowly before she said, "What about us?"

"What us? What are you talking about? Angie have you gone completely nuts!?" Shane blurted. He worried from Angie's bizarre behavior, what he might have done yesterday. "Angie," Shane tried to calm his tone, when he said this, "I barely had more than a few conversations with you yesterday morning and then after that I went to the bank, so I really don't know what—"

Angie cut him off, "No, not yesterday morning. I'm talking about what you said to me yesterday afternoon, right before we both got off our shift."

But, that was impossible. I wasn't even here yesterday afternoon. I was busy trying to stay alive surrounded by bank robbers, murderers, thugs and body-doubles. Shane mentally argued this fact knowing full well he couldn't tell Angie. He had wondered all day why nobody had asked him what happened or why he disappeared after a bank robbery took place in the same shopping complex.

I may have never returned from lunch for the second half of yesterday's shift, but someone who looked identical to me did and acted like it was just another workday. But, Cole was with me, ever since I absorbed him yesterday at the bank. Unless… The realization of what must have happened hit him like a wrecking ball. Shane suspected the frightening but obvious answer. *It must have happened at the bank.* He remembered thinking about going back to the bookstore right before the explosion that knocked him unconscious. *So, I can make more replicants of myself besides Cole?* If he had, Shane knew this could only mean one thing. There was another duplicate out there stalking Shane, and he was very close.

I can make more of them. I can make more of them and I released another one out into the world.

Slowly the pieces were falling into place of what took place here yesterday. This confirmed to Shane why it was that nobody at Brent & Nigel's had noticed his absence yesterday after lunch. Because to all of them he wasn't absent, he was right here with them working. And Ray's comment earlier about how he had spoken to the cops too; it all began to make sense.

I made the duplicate before going unconscious after the explosion in the bank. He must have picked up Cole's clothing and that means he also probably has Cole's gun that was left behind as well. Shane thought about this added bit of danger and the increase of his chances of getting himself killed that went along with this fact.

"But, if he went to work for me, and talked to the police for me, why is he messing with my life in these other ways? And more importantly where the hell is he now?" Shane was so lost in thought he hadn't noticed he was speaking these last words out loud.

"Who are you talking about? Who's 'he'?" Angie asked, nonplussed by Shane's odd reaction to this whole situation. Then, suddenly her eyes grew wide, and she yelled, "Oh no, I don't think so—I've had that one used on me before. 'Oh, Angie, look, you're really nice and all, but I'm gay.' Is that what you're trying to say to me, Shane Fisher? That you are now suddenly gay?"

Shane gently guided Angie towards the door saying, "Nothing, it's nobody. I guess it was my Mr. Hyde is all." He closed the door. Locking it on her scorned and confused face. With the office now empty Shane sighed deeply before finishing, "And it seems this particular Mr. Hyde likes to mess around with Dr. Jekyll's life for fun."

Shane sat back down in his chair, his head falling

heavily into his hands.

"I told you it was bound to happen at some point. Better sooner than later I say." Cole was speaking. Shane could sense the duplicate was standing in the room.

Shane sat, refusing to look up from his hands as he said, "Well, what exactly am I supposed to do about it? I don't know how to hunt down fugitive replicas of myself." Shane muttered hopelessly to Cole.

"Maybe you don't... yet? But we do." It sounded to Shane like Cole's voice had somehow multiplied. Many times.

His eyes shot open and standing in front of him was not only Cole but at least ten other naked duplicates crowding his small office. They were all smiling at him, waiting to see what he, the P.R.I.M.E., would do next.

I'll have to figure out what to do about the clothing issue, but strength in numbers can never be denied. Let's go find this trouble maker. Shane told himself as he stood from his desk. He walked towards the door absorbing each of his smiling doppelgängers as he passed them along the way.

The same smile began to play across his own face as he left the office.

EPILOGUE

Fragile awakened early, his sleep having been constantly interrupted by a combination of his mind racing and his joints and bones aching from the previous day. He got out of bed slowly and made some coffee. His tea would come later.

Fragile dressed in the golden morning light in his nicest herringbone tweed suit. It was old and faded like the man.

Fragile saw no real use in buying a new suit. He had nowhere to go in it. Since he took the child from Van and vowed to keep the P.R.I.M.E. safe from Director Gray, Fragile's life had been subjugated to the necessity of survival. A life of perpetual running and hiding and his own wishes and dreams from that day forward had simply taken a back seat. Fragile's defection from the Cabal's program and Director Gray was, after all, a life sentence. Or perhaps even more accurately a death sentence.

His age was worn on more than his clothing that day, yet still he glanced in the mirror before leaving the bathroom. Vanity always dies an ugly cruel death.

Once dressed, he finished his morning routine with a bite or two of a two-day-old dried scone to accompany the strong dose of caffeine.

Fragile was now ready for the day and set out on his morning walk. He hoped the crisp morning air would clear his head after the ordeal of the previous day's events.

The sidewalk Fragile walked along was broken, and the cane he had taken with him kept getting stuck in its cracks. But, this was the least of his worries that day.

Cole was gone, and someone new had taken his place, this boy–Shane Fisher.

He stopped then. Tears had filled his eyes. He found himself along the edge of the park near his apartment and decided to sit down a while on one of the nearby benches. Fragile felt a pang of familiar sadness. It wasn't the first time he had to get to know a new version of the entity, known as the P.R.I.M.E., and it wasn't like Cole was really gone. He was now included, a spoke on the wheel, of this new person, Shane Fisher.

Fragile found it interesting that every time he encountered a new P.R.I.M.E., that individual seemed to be lost. Almost as if they subconsciously knew there were missing pieces of themselves but had no way of ever finding them. In his own way, Cole had been no different from Shane, when Fragile had first found him. Cole's dark obsession had been a window into the soul of an incomplete individual.

Maybe that is what truly bothered Fragile. That even a radiant person like Cole, so confident and fearless, to ultimately be reduced to nothing more than an aspect of someone else's personality and identity. It made Fragile question what it was to even be a whole and complete person.

A life of purpose with passion and drive to achieve one's goals. Isn't that what we have all been taught to crave and strive for as human beings? What then truly defines us as individuals? The old man thought to himself as he sat quietly on the park bench. Yet, Fragile had never met a person alive more passionate or driven than Cole had been, so obviously, that was not enough.

However, a few things were very different this time. *Why was Cole staying around, still identifying himself as Cole?* It had come as a real shock for Fragile, when Cole had called, telling him that they had succeeded in re-covering the envelope and its contents. Normally, after a duplicate had been re-absorbed by a replica higher up the hierarchy of the P.R.I.M.E., he would completely lose his own past identity, accepting the fact that he was merely a permutation of the original identity, relinquishing himself completely to the new dominant being.

That is how it had always been in the past, however, this time was different, and Fragile knew it. It was almost as if this Shane Fisher was keeping Cole separate from himself. *But, why? Why would he keep Cole, a mere aspect or part of himself separate? Was this Shane Fisher's mind not stable enough and therefore showing some early signs of a psychological dissociative disorder forming?*

Fragile could not begin to imagine how confusing it would be for someone's mind to somehow conflate another person's past memories and experiences into his own. In the past, after the mind merging process had taken place, the new individual who emerged had completely and utterly incorporated those memories into his own, always relegating those memories to simple learning experiences and skill builders. But the

P.R.I.M.E., Shane Fisher, was for some reason keeping himself fragmented and separate internally.

Despite Fragile being one of the creators of the P.R.I.M.E. entity, and even after all of these years of observing him, Fragile still did not fully understand the processes that were taking place and was constantly surprised by the new and unusual abilities that manifested.

As a scientist, Fragile had a theory as to why this was the case. Fragile believed that the P.R.I.M.E.'s ability to split itself never meant for duplicates to be apart from the original for long periods of time, certainly not for decades. Perhaps, because with time and experiences came the need to make choices, and choices were what ultimately defined us as individuals. Therefore, the more time apart the duplicates spent from one another, the more independent and autonomous their minds would become. It was currently the best theory he could come up with at least.

When performed correctly, there is little difference between science and magic. Fragile smiled at the questions that this line of thinking always produced. In the journey of life, when one door is opened, revealing the mysteries of what had been previously hidden, more questions always seemed to arise. Crossing through one threshold leads to another door opening itself.

Fragile had never told anyone what Van whispered in his ear that day long ago. He never dared think about if he could help it. Revealing to the P.R.I.M.E. the truth about what it– what "He" was might be too much for anybody to handle. It could be catastrophic should the recursive system malfunction and Shane unknowingly turn himself into the most dangerous weapon of mass destruction ever created by man.

No. Better for him to figure out how to control his power first. Some truths are best unsaid. Fragile told himself, attempting to justify the omission he knew he was withholding.

But, now was not the time to ponder, it was the time to act. Arrangements had to be made, and Fragile needed to prepare this new P.R.I.M.E. even more quickly than in the past.

They had succeeded in intercepting the envelope and he had the true P.R.I.M.E.. The one that could make doppelgängers whenever needed. Now for the first time they had a weapon that perhaps could stand up to the power and vast resources of the Cabal. At least for now, the hunter had become the hunted and that only meant Shane and Fragile had a shrinking window of time to do something with the information. But all this really came down to how quickly Shane Fisher could learn to control these abilities. *Nine days is not much time at all.*

He stood up after a time and walked slowly towards the drop where Shane was supposed to have left the envelope.

The contents of the envelope disturbed him: Detailed information of all the current thirteen Directors of the Cabal and their designated meeting place was what he had expected to find. But, Fragile knew the location of the meeting being in Israel was far too significant to be a mere coincidence.

However, this detail was a mere trifle for what came next. One of the dossiers shocked Fragile so thoroughly that it was all that he could do not to drop the entire contents of the envelope to the ground.

Alive, but that's impossible. How could this be? She looked just as he remembered. In fact, as he had grown old over the years, it seemed she hadn't aged a day. There was no mistaking who it was.

Doctor Evangeline Murray.

ACKNOWLEDGMENTS

The hours of concentration and mental solitude become days. The days become months and eventually you emerge from the cave with some words on paper that (hopefully) tell an interesting story. The process is not pretty or exciting, but is always gratifying if you truly love the work. The book you are holding would not have been possible without the love, support and encouragement from the following individuals:

My mother Patricia, who has read more versions and edits of this story than anyone else, yet somehow remained enthusiastic and offered great suggestions throughout the process. My father Albert, who never failed to encourage me in my artistic, intellectual or professional endeavors, no matter how grandiose, whimsical or impractical. Thank you for teaching and encouraging me to dream big, but live even bigger. Jeb Corliss, for his keen insights into the world I am trying to construct for my readers and being an inspiration to let go of my fears. Hanna and Manfred Heiting. Hanna for inspiring me to be bold in my writing and never fear the development of my craft, but to embrace it. Manfred, my venerable sponsor, without whom this book aesthetically would not be what it is today. My (draft)readers Adina Gastelum, William Sutphen, Satie Gossett for their helpful suggestions and 'eagle-eyes' in spotting my grammatical shortcomings and flawed prose but somehow keeping faithful to my words and voice on the paper. Finally, thank you to everyone that I did not mention here. The list of which would be a book in itself and you already know who you are.